eternity

eternity

a novel

carlos

ISBN: 979-8-2181394-9-0 (Paperback)
ISBN: 979-8-2181995-9-3 (eBook)

Library of Congress Control Number: to come

Any references to historical events, real people, or real places are used fictitiously. Names, characters, and places are products of the author's imagination.

Book design by Glen Edelstein, Hudson Valley Book Design

Printed by IngramSpark, in the United States of America.

First printing edition 2023.

If you are a dreamer, come in,
If you are a dreamer, a wisher, a liar,
A hope-er, a pray-er, a magic bean buyer…
If you're a pretender, come sit by my fire
For we have some flax-golden tales to spin.
Come in!
Come in!

— *"Invitation,"* by Shel Silverstein

"I think it's all a matter of love: the more you love a memory,
the stronger and stranger it is."

—Vladimir Nabokov

prologue

they sit at a café on the Champs-Élysées. It is a typical spring day for Paris. Languorous lunches are prolonged with more wine and such, and the two of them blend in as if they quite belong, when in truth they don't. They have wine, but they don't drink. They have food, but they do not eat. They do not require such sustenance; in fact, they require little of anything.

She is attractive, with long, blonde hair, and she wears a white cotton dress, filled by the body of a typical twenty-eight-year-old. Lithe and sultry, she is pretty, but not beautiful. She blends in and does not attract attention.

He is good looking, tall, lean, and muscular. He wears a loose-fitting white cotton shirt and khaki trousers. He seems age appropriate for his partner, if that's indeed what they are. (They aren't.)

"I'm bored," the woman says.

He looks at her and smiles. "We can't have that."

"Shall we play a game?" she asks.

"I thought you would never ask," he responds jovially.

"One of yours paired with one of mine?"

He smiles. She smiles.

one

things are normal. normal in the sense that things are copasetic, not normal. What is normal? This, whatever this is, will have to do. He is going through the motions, things are less exciting, and he is alone. He works, he trains, he runs around. There is no off switch.

She is gone, although truthfully, he is not convinced she was ever here. Six years of trying to fit a round peg into a square hole and he finally figured out it would never be what he wanted it to be. Perhaps nothing ever is what we want it to be. Perhaps we are simply just survivors of settling for mediocrity.

They never lived together. It never even really came up. It should have, but it didn't. On occasion, she would ask him to run away with her. And he would laugh. Seriously? Run away with a person who doesn't seem to feel comfortable embracing progression? How does that work? It doesn't.

He would like not to be thinking about the failure, the waste, yet here he is. Misery, now *that* is as normal as it gets. In that case, he is rife with normalcy. Fuck it, all of humanity is suffering from an overabundance of miserable normal, or normal misery.

Routine seems to be the answer to it all, a distraction of what we must do. It's like muscle memory for the soul, assuming one's soul is vapid. His routine has been upended, albeit slightly, or is he not admitting it is more than that?

His dog is lying on the bed in the spot his girlfriend used to occupy on the rare occasion she would spend the night. The dog briefly raises his head to see what his master is up to—if perhaps, on the off chance, he may be fetching him a snack, but when it becomes clear that a snack isn't on the menu, the dog takes a whiff of his balls and subsequently cleans them with his long, pink tongue, which will undoubtedly be kissing his master later.

"Seriously?"

Saigon briefly stops mid-lick, as though he may have missed something important, but then resumes cleaning himself, adding his anus into the mix. His master showers, knowing he won't be able to be clean, not really.

The double showerhead rains down on him, and every drop that soaks him contains a memory. He sees her looking at him. The ghost of her haunts him in torturous, lonely whispers. He wants to let go. He has lied to himself, claiming that he has. The vulnerability seems to have entrenched itself deeper in his soul than he would like and is unlikely to endure. He guesses time will heal the emotional and physic wounds, but not today, or perhaps even in a thousand tomorrows.

Saigon is waiting when he emerges. He licks his leg to help with the drying process. It's cute, until he realizes that he had just been licking his balls and asshole quite thoroughly.

"Dude!"

Saigon puts his ears down in a submissive pose and pads off, probably going to clean himself further.

He dries himself and dresses, jeans and a T-shirt. Such is the business-casual life of a creative. He can't imagine being stuffed inside a suit all day working set hours. Yeeeshh, no thank you.

In the kitchen, he makes Saigon's breakfast and then sits at his desk, in the adjacent office. His morning ritual includes being lazy and procrastinating before he works. He tells himself it is work to a degree, but it's unadulterated laziness.

He is a story hunter. He hunts story. This is the general pitch as to what he does and who he is, but the truth is, he is a thief. He doesn't steal objects; he takes the emotions and experiences of others, some people he knows, some he doesn't. Of course, he borrows from himself a lot, too, but that can hardly count as thievery.

He has heard there are only seven original stories in the world, and perhaps that is accurate, but he is not buying. To him, story is like a fingerprint: sure, some are similar, but everyone has unique experiences. He credits perspective. Two people can see the same event yet recount it in completely different manners.

He teaches a writing class. Often, his students pitch their story, claiming they aren't writers. He always responds with the fingerprint argument: perspective is unique. The difference is craft, practice, and the balls to finish. Athletes practice, and craft is no different.

He is sure people wonder: if he is a thief and a story hunter, why not steal from the students who don't seem to care about the thievery anyway? It's a good question, but he finds it harder to write something that doesn't occur to him organically. Suggesting it is creative death. Of course, if he is paid to write some other story than one that had its genesis in his brain, he adjusts.

He is working on a screenplay. It's about a chemist who, at the turn of the century, fought for labeling of ingredients and overall food purity. He ended up with what would become the modern-day FDA, but not after a lot of pushback from the food and alcohol industry, who would use ungodly preservatives and chemicals to ensure a profit. He is struggling with the research, ready to abandon ship. He rarely starts and stops, but the chemist had test subjects who he intentionally gave the preservatives or chemicals he suggested were harmful to everyone except the manufacturers. That's the story—the volunteers who got sick for the betterment of humanity. The issue is there is little to no record of these men. He doesn't know how to pivot away from it, so he starts something else, a book.

This is his baseline, his norm. He needs to put something on a page. It is likely to be shit, yet it is something. Shit that may turn less shitty, or even good. He needs to be producing something or the fear of total creative paralysis may set in.

He is grateful to have a norm of any degree. He feels off, relieved, but off. He wonders if it may be the newfound singleness. He wonders if in the wasted time; he could have gotten another degree or watched two Summer Olympics. Had something to show for the time. He is frustrated with that. He blames himself, but still, the oasis of a creative burst staves off the annoyance of lack of personal norms. He knows that he is jumping ship on a project. He decides to tell himself it is a delay, buying time, but that is bullshit. The plus is that he has pivoted, didn't stop creating, but the truth is that, somehow, he is lost.

two

she looks at her client, who has said something that has gone unheard. She smiles and nods, faking her way through as much as she can. It works. The client pays and leaves, nothing amiss. She relaxes, takes off her mask. She can breathe real air until the next asshole shows up and the process starts again.

She is late twenties, attractive, Eastern European. Been in the county for years, although, if she had it to do over again, she wouldn't come at all. It is too late now: she has been gone too long to go back. Her life is entrenched. She has applied for citizenship but isn't convinced she wants it. She isn't convinced she doesn't want it, either. She isn't convinced of anything other than she would like a drink and not to be at work.

The fantasy of getting good and snoggered ends when the next client arrives, and the mask goes back on. This happy, happy face should probably get more credit for her repeat business.

Underneath the mask, she is feeling out of sorts. This isn't unfamiliar, not that anyone would really know other than her and maybe her friend. With him, she says how it is. They share a distaste for humanity. Maybe she will text him later.

The mask she is wearing itches, metaphorically speaking, that is. She is all smiles, chatty, pretending to be happy to see her client—a "friend"—after a month's time, when in truth, this is nothing more than a transaction. She doesn't feel respected. These bitches show up twenty to thirty minutes late and don't even apologize. Her time has no value to them, unless said time is spent making them more beautiful. It is all just superficial—they will always be ugly inside. No amount of time or primping will ever be able to fix that.

Her mind wanders while she chats, and she tries her best to make this bitch prettier than she was when she came in. The client is droning on and on, complaining about her husband and kids, but she seems very happy with her lover. She smiles at the client, not because the woman is happy with something, but because the lover is a busy boy—she knows of two other clients he is spending time with. It is a small community, where most people know of each other but not well enough to be aware they share the same gigolo. Of course, she won't be the one to tell them. She enjoys the power she has with all the information, and given her resentments, it is all for the best. Without the power, she may just feel like taking her mask off and murdering them.

Her phone pings, and she looks down quickly. She doesn't realize it, but she is smiling. The client notices and remarks on it, of course. It's her fault. She has bred this familiarity, and now the chickens are home.

"New boyfriend?"

She wonders if it is meant to be bitchy. She dates often, but it's not her fault she is picky. She wants what she wants and she will find it eventually. At least, that's the narrative she's spinning.

"Second date, but I like him." She says it and then realizes she should not have.

The client smiles as though she is happy for her, but she doubts she is, or maybe she just believes all her clients are entitled assholes.

"Oh-la-la, where is he taking you?"

"He didn't say."

And then she gets nervous—*he DIDN'T say*. She wonders if

she will have to make plans for them. She wishes she didn't have to, but now she thinks she should to avoid certain awkwardness.

The client is talking, but she isn't registering the words. Instead, she wonders if she should be seeing this guy if he doesn't make the plans for them. It isn't a good start, really. If he is phoning it in now, what will happen in a year?

Dating isn't easy. She is pretty, smart, and she is a pleaser. None of that matters, it seems. It's probably better to be a bitch. She gives too much and is probably taken advantage of as a result. But she won't change, despite the heavy flow of anguish it causes her. The right one will appreciate and love her. She can't stop now; he is out there. He must be.

three

the gym is his solace. He lets out all sorts of emotional crap on the weights and gets the bonus of feeling and looking better in one fell swoop. Except, he and his ex used to train together, and he is always dreading the possibility that he may run into her. It isn't that he doesn't care, or that things ended badly, but seeing her would dredge up unwelcome feelings he would rather not have. He desperately needs the release that training provides.

He has headphones in as he tries to focus on squats. It isn't so simple. Since he is a regular, he knows everyone, at least by sight, most by name. There are waves, fist bumps, conversations that last too long to have an effective session afterward. He does his best not to make eye contact. He just wants to load plates and tire himself out. Of course, he knows the gym is a social scene. He has met plenty of people there; he just doesn't want to linger.

He is adding weight to the bar when his eye catches something that makes him bristle in annoyance. There is a woman, probably mid-twenties, perfectly quaffed, setting up her phone on a tripod to video herself training. This Instagram world we live in makes him consider hara-kiri right there on the training room floor. She looks at him and smiles.

"Hi," she says.

He manages a wave, despite his internal protestations. She *is* attractive, with a great body. But the mentality is killing it for him. It's not like he doesn't have an Instagram account despite being older, but running into these self-obsessed people who are constantly wearing masks and facades is beyond frustrating.

He returns to squatting, but he finds himself checking her out in the mirror despite the annoyance. He quickly becomes frustrated with himself, as well. He finishes the set and drinks from his water bottle.

The Insta-chick approaches him, thrusting her phone in his direction as she does. He takes it instinctively. "Can you vid me? I can't get the tripod angle right."

"Sure," he says, dismayed.

He does as she asks, battling substantial self-hatred as he films her tight ass doing dead lifts.

"Thanks," she says as she collects her phone.

He nods and goes back to making his own ass and legs fabulous, but he notices Insta-chick stealing glances.

He rushes through some brief conversations as he leaves; it's all cursory bullshit, which he can't stand. He would rather have one substantial conversation a year than babble in small talk daily. He manages to endure and survive long enough to get out into the parking lot. It feels like he can breathe again.

The lot is small and full. The gym, by contrast, is huge and somewhat empty. He gets to his car, opens the door, and tosses his gear on the passenger's seat. He hears a light moan. When he looks around for the source of the sound, he spots Insta-chick in the car parked next to him. She's rubbing one out right there, her window open. He watches for a moment, incredulous.

"You can watch. In fact, I'd like it if you did."

It is hard not to smile. He is a voyeur, and watching isn't entirely unpleasant, albeit unexpected. He leans into the window and encourages her lascivious behavior. She watches him watching her, and her hand moves faster and faster until she explodes in a certain sound and fury. He looks around, surprised she didn't acquire more fans.

"I can suck your cock."

"I'd like that, but I shower at home."

"Invite me over," she retorts.

He thinks about it briefly. He values privacy, but being newly single, he values getting blowjobs from random chicks, too.

"Follow me?"

She smiles and nods.

He drives slowly, loins tingling with anticipation of some strange, mind tingling with trepidation. He looks in the rearview, both wanting and not wanting her to be there. He feels no commitment, so having impromptu sex with a stranger works just fine, but after having a girlfriend, it is also unfamiliar territory. He vaguely contemplates pulling over and telling her he has something to do so she won't learn his address, but next thing he knows, he is pulling up his driveway.

He jumps out of the car, and she parks next to him. "Nice house," she says.

"Come on in."

She follows him in, and he watches as she seems to do a baseline assessment of what he may be able to provide or offer.

He leads her through the kitchen and offers her a water, which she takes. She looks at him with her dark brown eyes. She touches his arm.

"I'm going to hop in the shower," he says.

"Conserve water?"

"What?"

"Can I shower with you?

"Oh, uh, sure."

He goes with her into the bathroom with the dual shower heads, and he turns on both. He watches as she takes off her clothes. This is really happening. He follows suit and both get in.

"I don't even know your name," he says suddenly.

"Names are unimportant. We are all just pawns in a game."

He thinks to protest, but she kneels and takes him in her mouth. Apparently, the part of him that wanted to personalize and humanize could be killed off easily enough by a skilled blowjob.

When they get out of the shower, she is drying off when she says, matter of fact, "If you have some cocaine, I will let you fuck my ass, bareback."

"Just weed I'm afraid," he responds nervously, wondering what bareback depravity she will let him do for that.

She seems disappointed, and to a degree, so is he, realizing that having anonymous sex with a stranger is probably an act of self-hatred. If his drug habits extended to blow, he wondered if he would be engaging in more salacious acts. He chuckles, knowing full well he would be.

"I can smoke, but no bareback. My boyfriend would be pissed."

"Yeah, I could understand that."

He grabs his vape pen and turns it on before handing it to her.

"Not going to smoke with me?"

"If I do, I won't get anything done."

"You used to work out with a woman, very tall and athletic."

He nods.

"Now you train alone and let strange women blow you?" she says, exhaling a massive cloud of smoke.

He shrugs, "I am pro blowjob. What can I say?"

"She's not your girlfriend?"

"No."

"Well, you looked like a couple. I was jealous you guys trained together. My boyfriend is a lazy fatass."

He wants her to leave and regrets sharing his weed. Ironically, as he has that thought, she hits the pen again.

"I like training alone. I like being alone in general," he admits.

"Don't be a dick, dude. I just drank your cum and didn't want to know your name. Kinda ideal, no?"

She has a point.

"I didn't mean . . ."

She hands him back the pen and starts to walk away but stops, spanks her ass, and says, "Next time, have a bump for me and you can have this."

He smiles and nods. He may want a next time.

four

the date isn't going well. The date isn't going at all. She is sitting at the bar of the restaurant *she* suggested and where *she* made the reservation. She'd been sitting there for twenty minutes. She wants to text again but does not want to seem too needy. It's too early for that. She doesn't want to expose her codependency too soon, but perhaps she has let herself slip and has scared him off prematurely.

Three assholes at the opposite end of the bar ogle her. They are wild dogs running in a pack—*fucking animals.* She feels their eyes beating down, as if the weight of all of them at once are on top of her.

She is wearing a bright yellow dress, the contour of her body is easily seen, and undoubtedly the dogs have had their glimpse, but it wasn't for them. It was for *him,* and he isn't around to reap the benefit.

She has been doing this a lot lately. Dating. She has also done a lot of failing. Her friend says it's the nature of the beast. Apps allow more connections, he tells her, and that makes it great and not so great all at once. It skews to the guys that want to hook up, he says. She knows he is right, but she can't help it. It is efficient in that she hasn't the time to meet people old school, and even if she had, she wouldn't. People don't approach her, and she, of course, won't approach anyone. That won't be changing, certainly not from her end.

Then she realizes that she'd met her friend that way. He had just come up to her at the gym one day. Maybe that's why she appreciated him; he had been able to move past her defenses with ease. He had told her that she'd been the one to wave him in, but she didn't remember it like that. Still, he came, and she was glad he did. He had become her best friend, and he would be the shoulder she'd cry this latest romantic failure onto.

One of the pack approaches her. She looks at him, mask on, and gives a slight smile. It isn't the attention she wanted but it's attention nonetheless.

"Are you waiting for someone?" the wolf asks.

She considers him. He is tall and slender, not entirely unacceptable.

"I'm not sure," she says coquettishly.

He smiles and sits next to her. "Your drink seems low. What can we order you while you may or may not be waiting?"

Okay, slightly charming. "It's a margarita."

He orders her a drink and one for himself. He asks about her, which is nice, and she allows it. He is getting the attention meant for someone else. She is getting the attention she wants and deserves. He is flirty, and she gets goosebumps when he slides his hand onto her bare arm.

Fuck.

She looks at her phone. There is no text from her planned date. But her substitute is pressing all the right buttons.

"Did you drive?" she asks.

"Huh?"

"You have a car here?"

"Oh, yes, I did."

"What kind of car is it?"

"It's a Jeep, why?"

"I was thinking about getting one. How about you show me?"

"Now?"

"Now," she says as she drains her drink.

She fucks the guy in the parking lot. Right there, for anyone to see. She hopes the asshole who stood her up sees it, but she knows he won't. The windows are fogged, and the sex is uncomfortable and sloppy. She feels terrible after. She doesn't know why she did it. *Was it some sort of revenge sex? Or did she just want to feel wanted?* She theorized that she had temporarily filled the chasm left by the asshole who'd stood her up.

She would have to be tested for an STD and get a pregnancy test. What *was* she thinking? *Stupid, stupid, stupid.*

"Can I get your number? That was hot." the unwanted asshole asks.

"Fuck off," she says as she jumps out of his Jeep.

She walks off into the darkness, swaying as she goes, knowing the animal is watching. She acts like she doesn't give a fuck but a category-five disaster hurricane is brewing inside her.

five

"i had sex with some guy in a parking lot. I didn't even know his name."

"Okay, I guess that's kind of understandable," he says to comfort her.

"And the asshole I was supposed to see fell off the planet or something. I really liked him."

"I don't know where you find these guys."

"The apps," she responds.

"Maybe give those a break for a while. Meet someone old school. Don't let the dating apps do the work. It makes guys lazy."

"Where?"

"I don't know, the gym? A bar?"

"The last guy I talked to at a bar got laid five minutes later."

"Good point. How about holding off on being such a slut?" She laughs. He follows suit.

"You always make me laugh. Thank you."

"I have a genius sense of humor, and I am also pleasant."

"You are the biggest bitch I know!" she teases.

"Pleasant! You want to grab dinner soon?"

"Sure, I don't think I will be having any dates for a while."

"Oh, please, who are you kidding?"

"Ugh, I need a break."

"You say that after every asshole!"

"I love that you know me but hate it sometimes, too."

"I understand. You busy Friday? There's that place I've wanted to take you to right by your work. Plus, it can be a rare Friday you keep it in your pants!"

"Fuck off," she says laughing.

"Fine."

"Friday is perfect."

six

the insta-girl is blowing him again. She seems to really enjoy it. He is holding her head down, making her gag a little before letting up for air.

"You like it rough? Mmm," she purrs.

He grabs her hair and is harder on her now that it appears she has given the go ahead. She gags more, and he smiles like the sick fuck that he is. He has come to discover that he likes creating pain sexually. He hasn't had any complaints, quite the contrary.

He is turned on by the dominant/submissive routine. He finishes quickly.

"That was hot," she purrs.

He smiles.

"Find me some blow and this can be all yours," she says, slapping her ass.

He doesn't know where to find her cocaine, but the idea of her submitting further definitely entices him.

"I wouldn't know where to get that. Sorry."

"What if I do?"

"I can pay for it, and we can have some anal?"

A degenerate smile crosses her face. "Sure, I can live with that. . . . I saw her the other day."

"Who?"

"The one you used to train with. To be honest, I got a little jealous."

"You did?"

"Yeah, I mean, I thought of you touching her, training with her, fucking her."

Jesus. This is more advanced lunacy than I originally believed.

"I thought you had a boyfriend?"

"Don't remind me. I like you better. You're nice, and your balls don't stink."

"You are a really beautiful woman. You can get any guy."

"I said I like you!"

He wishes he hadn't just seen *Fatal Attraction*. He assumes, and rightly so, that he needs to be delicate here.

"You flatter me."

"Fuck me bareback. Cum inside me."

No, no, no. How the fuck did I get on this crazy train all of a sudden?

"That sounds hot, but I have a doctor's appointment. I have to leave soon."

The Insta-chick has a hangdog expression.

"Next time!" He encourages her, knowing if he is lucky enough to get her out of the house at all, there will be no next time. "Let's walk out together."

seven

she is mad at herself. This was stupid, and now she'll pay the price, she is sure of it. What was she thinking? A little drunk and pissed from the lack of attention to risky, unprotected sex? If she's lucky, she will have only contracted something she can get rid of and not pregnant. She already has two kids she couldn't handle.

She is lost. Lost in whatever life has become, losing it, and this is what she is doing to manage. It's a clusterfuck of a hurricane from the depths of the soul. Does everyone do this? She needs help, but right now, she needs luck that she didn't hurt herself.

After a blood draw and urine collection, she sits quietly in the clinic as the woman examines her. She doesn't move but is squirming inside. The nurse asks her to lay back, and she complies silently. She stares at the overly institutional gray paint on the clinic's ceiling, thinking there should be a mural or something cheerier.

The nurse takes the standard fluids from her, does a swab and a smear. *The smorgasbord of slutdom*, she thinks. *This woman must think I'm a whore*. And then she wonders if she is. The nurse leaves with all of her samples.

She gets dressed. She feels worse now, and when she wonders why, she knows it's because she won't be able to be blissful in her ignorance. She's too smart for that. She wants to deal with her problems; she just wishes she wasn't always the root cause of them.

Such is the human condition. We make mistakes, and some of them we own.

She leaves the clinic, hoping that her lack of bliss won't ruin the rest of her week, or life. There's a bar next to the clinic, and she wonders which was there first, and if the placement of either or both establishments has been purposeful.

It is two o'clock in the afternoon, but she goes into the bar anyway. It is fairly empty aside from people sharing a mammoth plate of fries. She sits at the bar, and the bartender takes her margarita order. He is tall and flirty, so she doesn't order the fries that she wants. She orders a salad.

A text comes in from her friend asking what time he can make a dinner reservation so he can take her out. She smiles. She likes the way he operates. She wishes some of her romantic choices made the same effort.

"Good news?" The bartender catches her smiling as he delivers her drink.

She doesn't answer right away. She thinks on it. "Yes, I suppose it is."

He lingers a bit, flashing a big smile, perhaps testing to see if she may react in a way that will green light him to flirt on. She does not. She buries her face back in her phone and sips her drink.

"Let me know if there's anything else I can get for you," the bartender says before tossing his bar rag over his shoulder and walking off.

She looks at the text from her friend and briefly thinks they might make a good match. Then again, years of friendship has left them both overexposed to each other's secrets, and her thought flies away as if it had never entered her mind at all.

She texts him back to tell him what time she's done. He responds almost immediately, which garners a smile he will never know he elicited. He takes care of her in a way she likes very much.

When her salad arrives, the bartender doesn't try to talk to her. He sees he won't get anywhere; she doesn't even look up from her phone. She texts and drinks, finally noticing that her salad arrived. She takes a few bites and decides that, aside from the drinks, not much good can happen at a bar.

eight

they are the same, and still in Paris, although now they sit at a table at night under the Eiffel Tower. They are playing chess. It is odd because they look at each other, rather than the board, and the pieces move despite the fact that they do not touch them.

It is a beautiful spring evening in Paris. Occasional people pass by but don't pay any mind to the unconventional couple that play an unconventional game.

The woman looks at the man and smiles. She moves one of her pawns without touching the board. He counters with the same.

"So, it has begun," he says.

"Yes," she answers almost coquettishly.

"Rules?"

"No, that makes it boring."

"Not necessarily," he interjects.

"We need to add in challenges. It will make interesting."

"Please, humanity is so predictable. They all engage in the same self-destructive behavior."

She scoffs at the same time one of his pawns is eliminated by one of hers as if it were never there.

"That was a nice move. I didn't see it coming," he admits.

She rolls her eyes. "No, of course you didn't."

He smiles. She smiles, and as she does, she wonders if he let her know he was unprepared on purpose. She thinks he will be tricking her in the game they play with human lives, too, and that notion grows exponentially when he skillfully takes her bishop. She *was* set up.

He looks at her, his smile changing to a smirk.

"What have you in mind?"

"What don't I have in mind?"

She nods, and he returns the knowing look. She thinks to herself carefully so he won't hear her, but she never is so sure, given the way they are apt to operate.

"What is the end game? Success? Or crash and burn?" she asks.

"I do appreciate a good crash and burn, but they all end like that, don't they?"

"Almost always," she admits.

"So, you don't believe in their ability to love?"

"I believe they love. It's the lasting ability I call into question."

"Fine, I will take success, you get failure. You should feel at home considering how you are losing our other game."

He frowns as she makes yet another move he didn't anticipate, winning the game. He second guesses himself. She has bested him in this, so . . . why not that?

nine

he parks on the street and walks to her work. He has been there before but not in a while. He forgets exactly where her office is, as it is located on the bottom floor of a residential property. He stands and looks at the building. Rather than go in, he texts her.

"I'm outside, remind me what number."

"Just finishing up, be right out."

He is surprised at how fast she responds. He is prompt as always, but maybe she was waiting for him to forget his way around her work. He leans against a stone wall and procures his pen. He vapes the sweet taste of the marijuana before anyone notices. He doesn't want *her* to notice for some reason despite the fact he is fairly certain she knows he smokes.

He puts the pen away, and as if on cue, he hears the click of high heels on pavement. He chuckles to himself; she is always put together just so. He turns to see her. She is a blonde now. The last time he saw her, she was a brunette and her hair was longer. Regardless, she looks good to him, better than he will likely ever admit.

"Look at you all blonde and fluffy!" he teases.

They both laugh as they embrace. She kisses his cheek, and they walk off together, like they somehow belong in that time and space.

The restaurant is a quick walk away. He asks for a table in the back, and they order the same spicy margarita.

"You're staring," she says once the waiter leaves.

He brushes his fingers over her hand. "And?"

She shifts in her chair. "You usually look, but it's just different somehow."

"You are hot. Why wouldn't I look?"

"Because we're friends. It's inappropriate."

"Oh, I wasn't told I had to behave."

She smiles. He is always flirty, but this seems different. He moves his hand away when the margaritas arrive. They drink, and he orders for them without asking what she may want. She likes this. He knows she likes this.

"You have never eaten here?" he asks.

"No."

"I think you'll like it. The food is good, the drinks too,"

She sips her margarita. "This is good, nice and spicy."

He likes that she shares his taste for heat and also that she lets him order, curate the experience. He touches her hand again.

"What are you doing?"

"What?"

"You are coming on to me more than usual."

"And?"

"It's weird. We are friends."

He holds her hand, and she doesn't protest. She looks at him, and now she's thinking about him in ways she would prefer not to admit she has done before.

"We are friends," he admits.

"You're acting different."

"Am I?"

"You have a girlfriend."

"I told you that's over."

"Yeah, it has been 'over' what, a billion times before?" she asks sardonically.

"This is different."

"It always is."

They laugh.

"Another drink?" he offers.

"Is that a real question?"

They laugh again. They laugh a lot. They share the food and drink more drinks. It isn't a date, but to the casual observer, it is, and it appears to be a good one.

They walk outside, in lock step with each other, and he stops. She stops. He throws her up against the wall and kisses her passionately. He likes it. She likes it.

"Where are you parked?"

She takes his hand and they walk.

They get to her car, and he kisses her with purpose again. He stops and looks at her. They have obvious chemistry. The kisses are passionate, and if you were a voyeur passing by, you would undoubtedly watch what was unfolding.

He feels her breasts. They are firm and more wonderful than he had imagined. She pushes him off her. They are both breathing hard.

"What are you doing?" she asks him.

"I think that's obvious."

"I'm not sure if this is okay," she says, wondering why she would say such a thing when she likes him touching her.

"Feels more than okay."

She laughs. He laughs. He pulls his hands away and looks at her.

"Thanks for dinner" is all she can think to say.

He says nothing, just wears a sly smile and gets out of the car.

She watches as he walks off into the night. She is breathless. He, too, is breathless, but neither of them will let the other know it.

ten

she is thinking about him. She doesn't want to, but she is. She needs a distraction from this. She tells herself she should go on a date or something, and then she wonders if this is to prove something to herself.

He has a girlfriend.

He just wants to fuck me.

It will mess up the friendship.

He is going back to her, he always does.

She parks the car when she gets to work, and it makes her mildly annoyed that she reminisces about how he kissed and touched her in this very parking spot. She feels warmer than usual, and her legs tingle, and as she gets out of the car, and feeling off, touches her jeans and confirms what she already knew. Fortunately, she has a change of clothes in the car, and she grabs them and rushes to the office hoping she can change before her first client comes through the door.

She feels slightly embarrassed to be thinking this of her friend, and a bit more embarrassed that she was so turned on by the notion. She wonders what he's thinking.

Ugh!!!

She needs not to have him on the brain. She wants not to focus on him.

Date, for fuck's sake. Go on a date.

"Date?" her client asks. "You have one? Who is he?"

She is so distracted she didn't realize she was talking to herself as she entered the office. She puts on her game face and hopes she can concentrate on work.

eleven

he stares into the mirror at the gym, doing curls. The Insta-chick is there. He knows she can see him, but hopes she gets it and won't make things awkward and talk to him. She seems more interested in filming herself than anything else, thankfully.

He puts down the dumbbells, taking his eyes off her only briefly, yet in that time, she ninjas up to him.

"Hey!" she says.

He points to his earbuds, pretending he hasn't heard her. He does his best to act surprised.

"There you are!"

He smiles as wide as he can. She crosses her arms.

"I texted you," she says.

"You did?"

He stands silently, hoping she'll leave. She doesn't.

"I asked you to hang out. I miss you."

He looks around, hoping no one has heard her say that.

"Oh geez, I have been having issues with my phone."

"Technology . . ." she says, trailing off

"Right!"

He puts his earbuds back in and grabs the weights again. More curls. She doesn't leave as she has been cued to do. He knows she's there but doesn't look despite being utterly perplexed that she hasn't gotten the obvious hint.

He puts the weight down, and she touches his arm—a gentle reminder that she still exists. He feigns a smile and removes his buds again, trying not to give away his annoyance.

"I could hang out now," she says

"Oh, man, I wish I knew. I have a work thing."

She nods with apparent disappointment. He walks away, giving the obligatory wave, hoping she will catch on.

When he gets to his car, he texts her. Says that he enjoyed dinner. He looks at his phone to see if she responds expeditiously, but when she does not, he starts his car and drives off.

He pulls into his garage and looks at the phone again. There are texts but not from her. Naturally, the Insta-chick hits him up. Why is it always the one you don't want that wants you? He wonders why humanity is so sick. He wonders why *he* is so sick.

Just let it go…

Why would you even start with her?

And he thinks on it, *why?*

Then it hits him. She cares. She has always cared. *I am drawn to women who care. For fuck's sake, who wouldn't be?*

Stop thinking.

Stop analyzing.

He closes his eyes as if to shut up the voices in his own mind. They are incessant.

But his mind does shut up as his phone beeps. It's a text and it's from *her.*

He smiles, and his mind quiets down.

twelve

the woman is talking to her, but she isn't listening. She appears to be but is not. It registers that the woman is talking, and she nods and looks the part, yet does not hear.

She thinks she has decided to have sex with him. It would be an improvement over her last anonymous lover. Why not *him*? He is older than she is, and she is curious about that, and every time he is off with his on-and-off girlfriend, he comes on to her hard. It isn't that she doesn't like it, but she doesn't trust it. But why not see? Just dip a toe into the water to check the temperature.

I'd like to take you out for your birthday, LMK when we can plan something.

She doesn't send the text. They always have taken each other out for birthdays, so she is uncertain why she feels this is trepidatious. He started the tradition, although she didn't accept the offer right off. Having a male be only a friend was unprecedented for her. She was worried that the friendship would be unacceptable to prospective suiters, then again, given her luck, she wouldn't have to worry about that in the long run. She hadn't been in any semblance of a relationship since their friendship commenced, with one mistake of an exception.

That exception definitely was against the friendship. She brushed it off at the time. She found it interesting that the exception was insecure about her only male friendship, when she herself thought nothing of it at the time, other than she enjoyed it.

It no longer mattered; the exception lasted one tumultuous year, and her friendship had endured, and was it growing into something else? She let her mind rewind to how he had grabbed her and kissed her. When she snaps out of the memory, the woman she had been not listening to is standing and staring at her impatiently.

"What?" she asks

"I am waiting for change, still," the woman bitches insensitively

She smiles and hands her back her crisp hundred-dollar bill.

"No," the woman says, "I want change."

"It's not necessary," she tells her, matter of fact.

"I don't understand."

"I'm not interested in having you as a client," she says, opening the door.

The woman instinctively scuttles out, albeit confused beyond her means. The woman stops and looks at her, as if expecting this to be a joke.

She closes the door on the addled woman, smiling contentedly as she does.

thirteen

he takes the shot and flexes a bit after draining the three-pointer as two opponents try and defend him. He has been on fire all game, and he feels like a pro. The shot wins the contest, and his teammates are full of high-fives, back and butt slaps.

He walks toward the door to the locker rooms.

"Hey, where ya goin'?" someone chortles

"You've had enough, I think," he says, turning around to see some disdain but way more smiles.

He changes his shirt in the locker room. He is loath to shower there. The things he has seen in the bathroom alone has permanently stomped the notion of putting his bare feet on the public tiles.

He senses someone staring at him and turns around but there is nothing but a bank of beat-up lockers, lonely and waiting for someone to fill them.

He finishes with the pseudo clean up and grabs his gym bag, heading into the main room on his way to being free of all the people and into the safety and solitude of his car.

As he's leaving, he gets that feeling again, as if someone is watching, some sort of ghoulish presence. It's odd, to be sure, and as soon as he is in the parking lot, he understands what he was feeling, and why.

His exes' car is parked in the lot. He does not want to run into her. Things ended awkwardly and he isn't ready. He was glad he didn't see her, but he did wonder if she'd seen him.

He hustles off to his car. He had wondered if she still lived in the area, she had always seemed to be on the brink of running off, and when he finally chose not to continue the toxic cycle of up and down, he had assumed she finally would execute her escape plan.

He *had* told himself that the ex was gone. Left. Clearly, he needed that for his own sanity, but now that he realized she was still in his orbit, he wondered if they could be friends. Then he considered if that were a wise choice. He'd been let down. He knew he wasn't perfect, but he'd given it all he had. He was always like that: it was all in or nothing.

Yet now things were in some sort of purgatory. He was relieved, in a sense, but they'd had some good times over the years. He couldn't help thinking about better days they had shared.

There really ought to be a manual.

He started the car to drive home thinking he should forget friendship, or perhaps any relationship, at any time. He wasn't so good at them, and years of failure hadn't helped him get any better.

I can just be a solo act.

It wasn't that he didn't like having a special someone, but with all his past someones, he had failed for various reasons, never quite being able to deal with his damage, her damage, or both damages. Years would go by, full of ups and full of downs, but they all ended the same way.

Being free had its benefits: no one to report to, endless lovers that could be interchangeable.

I got the life! Interchangeable lovers!

Eh, is it the life?

He thinks of her, then his ex, the Insta-chick. *Her. Fuck. Fuck. Fuck.*

In his car, he looks at his phone. As if divine intervention, he gets a text from her. He smiles. He looks at his ex's car and drives away from it. He hopes forever.

fourteen

they dance at a club, still in Paris. It is interesting to see, as they are somehow in sync with each other's movements yet never touch. The music is loud, pulsating, the smoke machines billow, and lights flash colors of the rainbow as couples both of same and opposite sexes dance together in pairs, or sometimes groups.

The pair never look away from each other. If they were to be observed long enough, it may seem as though they need to be tethered in a way no one can understand. But they don't need to, and no one can observe them anyway, at least with human eyes.

They speak without using their mouths, or any verbalization at all. Then, they nod at each other simultaneously and everything stops—as if someone pressed pause at the night club.

They, too, are motionless sculptures, until they aren't. They take each other's hands but do not touch, as if hovering is the way they connect.

"Who shall we choose?" the girl asks.

"I never know. They all are so boring," he responds.

"Same sex? Opposite sex?"

"As if it matters. They all fuck it up somehow regardless."

She smiles. He smiles.

They look over the frozen club-goers like they are shopping for fruit at a farmers' market. Occasionally, they stop and look at a couple, run their hands over their hair, or touch their skin, as if some sort of a litmus test.

"These all seem so typical. It will be over before it's begun," she tells him.

"You always know best."

"Then why do you wager with me?"

He smiles. She smiles. He shrugs, and her smile widens. He indulges her, and she likes it.

"We need to do something vastly different from our usual," she suggests.

"You know I will always agree to one of your challenges," he replies with a hint of snark.

"It alarms me when you become too agreeable."

"That's good. I can't have you too comfortable if I ever want to win one of our wagers."

"I suspect you of letting me win."

They look over some other couples, including two very pretty young men who are probably just going to fuck and never see each other again. Then again, it occurs to them that all these pairings are likely in superficial relationships.

"These just won't do!!"

"Agreed," he says.

"I want you to pick someone challenging, and I will choose someone in his orbit, and the game shall begin."

"You are letting me make the first move?"

"Why not? It's another challenge, but I won't make it easy. You must pick someone coming off a breakup. He needs *not* to be ready. And then I will come with someone who *is*, for him, but he won't know that, and maybe she shouldn't either!"

"Challenge upon challenge, I like it."

And as they leave the club, it is as if the play button has been hit and the bump and grind on the dance floor resumes without missing a beat. Only our ethereal friends are aware that anything has happened at all.

fifteen

his ex calls a few days before his birthday. She wants to take him out, but he has finally had enough. The bizarre secrecy, everything on her terms. It had been toxic beyond repair.

He politely declines the invitation. He tells her he doesn't want the same thing over and over again, but maybe they can be friends down the line. She asks if he's sure. He says yes, that they have different wants and needs and, while it works on some levels, fundamentally it does not.

The call ends with little fanfare. He tries to ask about her and how she is, but he is met with the same passive aggressive bullshit she has employed before.

It is odd, to be sure. She sounded upset that he wouldn't capitulate again. But it had finally run its course for him. Nothing was going to change, so why invest in redundant failure? How could she not understand?

She constantly said she didn't want to be judged, but how is it judgment? Hiding your life from a "partner"? After years of investing emotionally? Fuck that. Relationships are disasters waiting to happen. It's way easier not to deal with some other person's damage and built-in redundant bullshit.

Then again, meaningless sex with stage-five crazy women who think they can fuck their way up the quality of boyfriend ladder. . . . Seriously? Insta-chick offers to charge for a parking lot BJ? And then maybe date?

Perhaps a life of masturbation and porn will make things better. Lonely, yes, but is it better? *Sure as shit seems so. Yes, yes, yes.*

He wants to text his friend, but he is pretty sure he overstepped several boundaries the last time. They seem a natural fit in so many ways: ease of operation, communication, and when they kiss? There's no way she isn't tuned into the same frequency. But he has never pushed her. He has tested the water quite a bit, though. He has sort of taken what he could get, but then let it go if his footing seemed tenuous.

Then again, when in life isn't our collective footing on shaky ground? This was all new territory for him. He hadn't thought of it until now, but he had upset his apple cart, had begun floating without ballast in an ocean that was infinitesimally vast.

Who am I, and what do I want, and why is there so much fucking shit in my way while I figure that out and attempt to get there?

He stares at himself in the mirror, asking these questions, having no answers. Of course none come. Do they ever? But something is there. He doesn't see it, because what is there isn't visible to human eye, yet he senses it. That feeling of being watched.

He looks in the mirror. It's as if there is someone standing behind him, observing. He has often had this feeling when something spiritual or extra ordinary is happening. As a rule, he generally doesn't share these things, but when he has, the responses he receives are usually positive. Perhaps people are being polite, gracefully sidestepping the train to Crazy Town, or maybe they feel these things, too.

He's always thought the bathroom off the kitchen in his house is the haunt of an old woman. He is especially creeped out at night when he lets the dog out. Perhaps it is just that voice inside all of us that loves to create chaos. On occasion, he senses her so strongly that he doesn't dare pee, even when he really has to go. He prefers the safety, and the no-one-died-in-here feeling of the master bath. Yet when he does brave it, he feels as if she is passing through him, as if trying to get some taste of life that has long since eluded her.

Whatever he senses in the mirror isn't her, though. It feels like a spirit, maybe passing judgement on him or something. He isn't sure. All he knows is that he is being observed. He looks at the space in the mirror where he feels the presence, winks, and leaves.

He takes Saigon for a walk in the woods. There are trails and streams, places for a dog to explore and his human to get lost for a while. On occasion, he passes another soul who waves or gives a brief verbal acknowledgment. Most rather talk to Saigon than to him, and he is fine with that.

At one point, Saigon seems to have exchanged him for a woman hiking on her own. She laughs as the sleek black dog follows her. He suspects that she has packed a hamburger; the dog would go with any stranger bearing such gifts. It is quite touching when you think about it.

He calls Saigon and then sits on a bench that is conveniently waiting for him. Eventually Saigon comes leaping and bounding through the woods to his true master's orbit.

"Where have you been?"

The dog looks at him, probably telling him something that would really interest him if he were a dog, too. And with that, he leaps and bounds off again. The dog decides to make friends with an older couple, approaching them as though making an introduction.

"Great dog!" the male part of the couple says.

He is relieved that they are not admonishing him for having a dog off leash as some older people are wont to do.

"Thanks," and then he proceeds to answer all the questions that come about the dog. He really should just print pamphlets.

He keeps the courtesy going as long has he can. They are nice; it's not their fault he is antisocial. He fakes being a people person adroitly, after all, he has lots of practice. He finally edges away from them, but he notices something interesting: they are always touching. Small, light fingers on skin, as if they are constantly connected. For someone who didn't very much care for the species he belonged to, he was sensitive to the rare occasion human beings displayed their worth.

As he left, he wondered if a long-term connection was something he could ever achieve, or even actually wanted. Sometimes things look appealing from afar, but upon closer inspection, they're a no go.

He liked the idea of someone special, but then his track record seemed to indicate that maintaining the specialness of it was harder than it looked. There were no manuals for such things, and his relationship IQ seemed to be whatever the opposite of Mensa was.

It didn't matter. He was single again, free as a bird to do whatever he pleased and not have to worry about someone else's feelings or protestations. He liked being free, but it may just be nicer to be with someone special and still feel that same freedom.

He questioned his existence, life in general, the meaning of it all, and despite all the brain power, he had no answer as to what it was about. He just wanted to practice his art and have fun from time to time. It seemed simple enough, to be sure, but then why was he so bad at it?

sixteen

she is late. it isn't new, and it is unlikely to change. She is perpetually late. It isn't her fault exactly. There is always so much to do, and they never give extra hours in the day to do them.

It's always the days with the kids that seem like there aren't enough minutes in the day. It is compounded that she had them and not soon thereafter realized that the marriage wasn't what she had hoped for. Kids for a single parent can be a challenge, and she had been looking to fix her mistake ever since, although she didn't realize it. She just thought she didn't want to be alone.

She had planned to go to the gym, but if she did, she'll be late to work and then get home just in time to get up and start the next day. It's a never-ending cycle, even on days when she hasn't parental responsibilities.

She thinks she has had enough in the romance department. Fail, fail, fail and followed by meaningless sex, which she resents herself for after the fact.

He asked her why she does it once, after she confided in him, but she didn't know, and she told him that. She can tell him anything, and she usually does, judgement free.

She texts him and reminds him that she wants to take him out for his birthday. She asks where he wants to go and when. She catches herself smiling when he responds, and so a date is set. The date, though, is after his birthday, and she wonders who gets him on that day. Probably his on-and-off-again relationship that he doesn't seem to be able to navigate successfully.

She has told him she wished he would move on, and sometimes he says he will eventually, but then that day never comes. He has told her everything's eventual, but she will believe it when she sees it. He does come on to her when he says he's in an off part, but what guy wouldn't say that? She sees how he looks at her, but then again, she gets that from men and women.

It can be annoying. She doesn't mind when people look, but then on occasion, it's more than just subversive glance. There are catcalls, whistles, she once even influenced a small fender bender when the jackass driving the car was looking at her too long as she crossed the street, and he drove right into the car in front of him. The asshole even tried to guilt her into giving him her number. Instead, she gave a police report, but then the cop also asked for her number.

She bemoans to her friend, and he says that she should complain if no one is looking rather than the opposite. Looks fade, he reminds her, but she doesn't believe him. She will always be beautiful.

It won't happen to me.

She is right—it won't happen to her. Not anytime soon, that's for sure. She is young and beautiful and will remain so for the foreseeable future.

She fluffs herself in the mirror, not too much, but just enough. She is going to work not on a date. She wants to look good but not too good. The bitches that she services can't be outdone, that would be a mistake, even though—*mirror, mirror*—she is the fairest of them all. No, she must be pretty but not showstopping gorgeous. Pretty for herself, of course, but also for *them*. They are *that* superficial, yes, and she is smart enough to understand how the game is played.

Still, it is exhausting. She is always on the go. Drive here, drive there, kids, work, an occasional social life. *Is this all it is?*

In traffic, she scans the apps. So many guys are on multiple sites. She deletes her profile from one and almost hits the car in front of her because she's not paying attention. Before the delete, she sees that there are 556 messages for her. They can't all be from different men. She thinks about checking them and then remembers her behavior in the parking lot after being stood up, so she just erases any trace that she was there.

She repeats the process on two other sites, one she hadn't even been on in months, according to the log in-information. She closes the account and deletes the app. She kills the last one in the same fashion.

I'm done.

Again.

She thought about her behaviors with the digital dating. Up and down, down and up, and side to side were the motions of choice. It was out of control. Looking for love was a perilous and sick venture. She wondered who was even good at it. Fuck them, whomever they may be.

He had a suggested she try meeting someone the old-fashioned way. Apps made guys lazy. Leveled the playing field, is what he said. It did make things easier. Women on the apps invited the usual behaviors. Men were emboldened by the increased level of possible success. It made sense to her. He always made sense to her. She bit her lip absently, remembering how he kissed her. He just took what he wanted, and she liked that, a lot.

She finds herself thinking about taking him to dinner, and even though a date is set, she wishes it were sooner. Will he kiss her again? Or will he tell her he's gone back to his ex?

Ugh.

She doesn't want to be thinking about him like this. She mustn't. They are friends, and she can't risk losing that.

No, no, no.

Then, in a defiant move, she gets back on one of the apps.

seventeen

his ex calls, and when he sees the number, he ignores it. It isn't easy. For years he had tried, and for years he had failed. In the end, he realized what they wanted, and how they wanted it, was just not the same.

He listens to the message that she has left: she asks again to see him for his birthday. Then a text flies in, also from her, asking him to please call her.

It stings despite the fact he made a conscious choice. Why do choices have to be so difficult, especially with matters of the heart? Inevitably, one or both people get hurt.

Who is good at this?

It isn't him, and with his track record, it likely never will be.

Free agent. No more romantic fires. They burn too long, and the damage is irreversible. Worse yet, the burns sear you from the inside out, until your blood boils your bones, and you fall into an endless nowhere.

He thinks to call her back. Despite giving up on the romance, he did spend years trying to come to a different conclusion, but there was still a void. In spite of the fact he wished he didn't care, he was too sensitive and did. He didn't want to cause pain, but she had made it out like this was a surprise. Why didn't she know?

He looks at the contact number and almost pushes the call button, but in the end, he puts the phone down, calls Saigon, and they leave for the woods, phone safely tucked away.

In the woods, he thinks about what he will do for his birthday. He thinks about calling her, even though he agreed to a later date.

No, it's too much, what was he thinking?

He likes her very much, and he always has a good time with her, but was it so terrible to be alone?

He walks in the woods, Saigon padding along by his side as he thinks about it, coming up with little to no explanation. Saigon stops to watch as two squirrels appear to be fucking.

"Now that is the right idea."

The sleek dog looks at him as if in agreement before bounding at the rodents, breaking up their fun and sending them scampering up trees. Saigon stares up, as if to let them know he can wait them out if he chooses, yet he does not. Instead, he resumes his spot at his master's side as though he knows something his human doesn't.

He loses himself in his wanderings, and as he does, he realizes the irony.

We wander through life, having an occasional ballast, then we jettison. We let go in some way, shape, or form.

When he leaves the woods, he leashes up Saigon and realizes that he is crying.

He feels an epic sadness, not only for himself, but for the entire human race.

eighteen

they sit on the ledge of the Pont Neuf, legs absently swinging as the Seine flows beneath them. They don't look down, as if they are more there for the sound than the sight.

It is late at night, or early in the morning, depending on who you are. They are no one, yet also everyone, but regardless, sleep isn't what nourishes their life force. In fact, they don't require sleep at all.

One may wonder what they do, in fact, need. Truth be told, they require little to nothing other than each other to keep themselves from certain boredom that is common for such entities.

Yet that was about all that was common. It simply wasn't a word or notion suitable for a creature of this nature.

And if one wasn't certain of all this before, soon that will change when the ethereal creatures begin the game that they have been wanting to play.

The water in the river below them begins to swirl, as does the pair on the bridge above. The water rises up and makes what looks like a giant screen.

"You are ready to begin?" he asks.

"I cannot wait any longer," she responds.

"You pick, and I will follow."

"Ha! I wasn't asking for permission."

He smiles. She smiles.

The water flattens out, and it does indeed become a portal of sorts, through which they see a face.

"This is your selection?" he asks her incredulously.

"Yes, why not?"

"He is a mess, and how can you possibly succeed under such circumstances?"

"They are all messes, are they not?" she asks him.

He looks at the image in the water in front him. The guy is walking with a dog in the woods and seems normal enough. The creature senses something amiss, yet he cannot pinpoint it.

He wonders if he has been outsmarted, but then he smiles when he comes to his choice.

The water changes to a pinkish hue, and she sees the woman he has selected.

"You can't be serious," she chortles.

"I am."

"So, the game is afoot?"

"For the ultimate prize."

He smiles. She smiles.

nineteen

he sits alone at the bistro situated on the corner of the main street of the small suburb. It is a nice fall day, perfect really, a gentle breeze runs through the seventy-degree weather as small trees show changes in the color of their leaves.

It's all very lovely, and the moment isn't lost on him. He drinks in the bucolic beauty. He has been doing that of late, noticing moments. Someone suggested that he appreciate the now of things, rather than lamenting the past or being washed away in the anxiety of some horrible, possible future.

Of course, the demon that lives in his head loves to list what is wrong and fills him with anxiety-provoking whispers that pepper his mind.

Your work is terrible. You aren't smart enough to pull this off. She is just talking to you because she thinks you have money.

He is thankful when his hamburger arrives. *Food is the elixir of life*, he thinks as he looks at the caramelized onions and gooey melted brie mix oozing off the side of the burger.

"It looks amazing," he says to the waiter.

"You should know, you eat enough of them."

He laughs at the familiarity. Of course, the waiter is correct.

"I can't help it, best burger ever,"

The waiter nods and he is left alone to eat. He is no stranger to being out with himself, and it doesn't bother him. In fact, sometimes it is preferred. Company can often be dreary, and usually he can't wait until he can shed whomever he has committed to spending time with. Humans, as it turns out, are not his favorite species.

I should have brought Saigon.

He was going to go to a bar after, have a celebratory cocktail, but now he has decided against it, which annoys him further for not bringing the member of his preferred species.

He finishes the meal quickly and asks for his check and pays. He doesn't know why, but he no longer wants to be out in the world.

He gets home and is greeted by Saigon, always happy to see him.

Preferred species.

He rolls a joint and Saigon follows him out onto his deck. The loyal dog sits with his master, looking out into the night sky.

"Get me a beer boy."

The dog cocks his head then nudges his master's hand as if asking for further explanation.

"Fine, I will go."

He lumbers into the kitchen, and the dog pads along with him. He opens the fridge for a beer and sees the sorry cupcake he bought as a birthday cake. It is chocolate with chocolate buttercream. The effects of the smoke have kicked in, and he grabs it, puts in a bowl, and heats it. He adds chocolate ice cream.

Saigon looks to him as if to ask where *his* snack is. He responds by getting him a treat.

He opts out of the beer and takes the sweet birthday treat into the bedroom and watches TV. This is how it is, and maybe it is for the best.

He sits there watching some cooking show while his enhanced hunger enjoys the sweet dessert. He looks at his phone, little to no activity.

I am not so popular on my birthday.

He felt alone, he always did, and perhaps it was some sort of self-punishment. It was, in fact, of his own doing. He had offers to be taken out, but as he usually did, he had denied all his suitors. In fact, he only took his friend up on the birthday dinner.

Little did he know how things would change.

twenty

she texted him to ask if he liked a steakhouse that was on the water, and when he said he did, she made a reservation. He responded quickly, she liked that.

The dinner was still awhile off, but she was glad she had the plans all good to go. In the meantime, she was off to the city to meet a friend she hadn't seen in a while. She felt better for some reason; she was free in a way that she had not been until lately.

Perhaps it was the respite she allowed herself from dating. It stressed her out more than it yielded any romantic success. Who had time for it under such auspices?

She had entered a prelapsarian period, and it felt good. That's what mattered. She drove to Brooklyn to meet a friend. It was a beautiful fall afternoon. She parked the car and went to a restaurant that had a view of the bridge. The two women sat outside and enjoyed snacks and drinks. Her friend complemented her on her glow, saying she looked happy and healthy.

She smiled at the compliment. She felt good inside, and she thought she always looked good outside, but one can always look better. Perhaps the elixir for the toxicity of dating had power beyond what she as aware of.

They caught up and ate and drank, and her friend, a photographer by hobby, asked if she would like to go to the bridge and take some snaps.

Why not?

They walked along. Such a beautiful day to be out and about.

"Here is a good spot. Sit on the railing for me."

She looked around her, wondering why the spot was good, but she noticed immediately the iconic stone pillars of the bridge, coupled with the buildings of Manhattan in the background. She sat and looked about, drinking in the people, the perfection of the day. She didn't notice that her friend was taking pictures, which was for the best, as when she saw the pictures later, it all seemed so natural.

"Hi there."

A man had stopped and gotten off his bicycle, just to talk to her. The gesture was unexpected. She found herself smiling.

"Hi."

"Oh, do I detect an accent?"

Christ.

She nods.

"German?"

Is he joking?

She shakes her head.

"Hmmm . . . I'm not good with accents, but it's nice, whatever it is."

Thank God he's given up guessing.

She smiles, wondering what he wants.

"You live in Brooklyn?" he asks.

"No."

"A woman of few words. You are so mysterious."

She nods. He tells her his name; she tells him hers.

"So, it was nice talking to you, but my friend is waiting for me," she points to her.

He looks behind him and her friend waves. "Sorry, I didn't realize."

"You couldn't have, it's okay."

"Can I have your number? Maybe we can do something sometime."

He waits uncomfortably. She isn't sure. He isn't bad looking, but she has sworn off dating. Then again, in her head, she can hear her friend in her mind.

Why not try to date old school . . .

"Give me your phone," she tells the stranger.

The man almost can't believe his luck. He fumbles for his phone in his pocket, almost losing it over the bridge when it flies out. Fortunately, he catches it and hands it to her, trying to be cool about it.

She laughs, which is nice, and she gives him her number. She calls herself from his phone, so she knows who he is if he calls or texts.

"I will hit you up soon," he says, taking the phone.

He lingers a bit too long and finally moves off. Her friend comes over and they laugh together.

twenty-one

he is leaving the gym, and he senses someone looking at him, but when he turns around, he's alone. In his head, music is playing, and he wonders if the music somehow made him feel haunted. He removes the headphones to eliminate the eerie feeling. It does not work, but when he left the gym, he understood this feeling.

There it was, in the parking lot, again. The car he had been familiar with for failed years. He stood and looked at it, briefly wondering if she had seen him and just left him be. Or did she miss him in passing and didn't know he was there?

Should I go back?

He stares at the car, then at his car, then at the door to the gym. He feels panicky and soon realizes that he should get out of there as fast as he can.

He gets into his car as if his pants are on fire. He starts the car and wonders if she saw him running off in such an odd manner.

He doesn't want to see her, but he doesn't want her to feel alienated either. He would like to acknowledge her from a safe enough distance not to be sucked back into the vicious circle of relationship failure.

Distance was the key. He wondered what spell she had cast on him. Or perhaps it was his inability to give up. Either way, he knew distance, over time and proximity, was the safe bet.

When he gets home, he thinks about shooting her an email, but then thinks better of it. They belong to the same gym, so what? It was as if he wanted to solidify the rules of engagement. She had always found ways to pull him back in, although he realized it was probably just as much his doing.

Who the fuck knows?

He smokes a joint, which is odd. It is the middle of a weekday, and he smokes almost absentmindedly, as though his self-medicating response is on autopilot.

Saigon comes in from frolicking outside.

Left the door open?

He was bothered by the affect he was registering. He was sure it was normal, but it bothered him regardless.

He took a deep breath and started the shower. The hot water felt good on his throbbing head and achy body. The anguish and angst, combined with training, had taken its toll more than it should have. But he needed to wash it away, to be cleansed of it all, so he stayed under the water as long as he could take it.

After, he got himself dried and dressed, he left the house to get coffee. *Big mistake. Huge.*

Once inside Starbucks, he reminisced about how he first met his ex.

I am an idiot.

He wondered if the natural self-destructive nature of human beings was pulsing inside him unconsciously. He hated that about humanity, he hated it in himself. He wasn't a people person. He could appear to be, of course, that was one of many masks he wore. But deep inside, he loathed the species, mostly for stupidity, the redundant damage done, all the while pretending nothing was wrong. It made him mental. He made himself mental when his head wasn't in the game. And his head was not in the game, plus he'd decided to self-medicate.

Stupid, stupid, stupid.

He was just one of the same species he had learned to loathe.

twenty-two

she stares at the shoes, trying to decide if she likes them. They were shiny, glittered to the gills, as she preferred, but too much?

"Oh, I love those," a voice comes from behind her.

"I can't decide," she says, turning.

The saleswoman is there, wearing a fake smile. The feigned look is reciprocated with an equally, if not better, feigned happy face.

"Would you like to try them on?"

She wasn't sure, but she finally nodded. She didn't really have time, but she wanted something new, and when she thought about it, she realized she wanted something new for when she went out with him.

What she was feeling, she didn't want to feel. She was sensitive, but he was always there. He always listened and gave good advice, she cared about him, and she was pretty sure he cared about her.

She remembered a few years back when he texted her to wish her a happy birthday, and when he found out that she had no plans, he dropped everything and took her to dinner.

"Do you like them?"

"What?" she says, not realizing she had absently tried on the shoes.

"Is there another pair you would like to try?"

"I'm sorry, I forgot to eat this morning. I get spacey when not properly fed."

"That makes two of us. So, what do you think?"

She stands and walks around, admiring the way her feet fill the shiny shoes.

"I will take them," she says, handing the saleswoman her credit card.

The woman walks off, and she changes back into her original footwear. When she stood, she was a bit dizzy. She sat back down quickly. She takes a few deep breaths. Her phone buzzes with a text alert. It's him. She realizes that in the moment, that she sat she thought of him, wondering how he was, and then magically he texts. Perhaps it was just coincidence.

What else could it be?

The saleswoman comes back with her card and receipt. She thanks her for the business, smiles politely, and leaves.

She texts him back and says she is good, asks about him. It is cursory, but she wonders if there is more to it than that.

She stands again, sans dizziness, and walks to her car. In the parking lot, some guy driving by rolls down his window and whistles at her. She shakes her head in disgust.

What is annoying her now is the guy that catcalled her in the parking lot has come around again as she is getting into her car. She looks at him in disbelief. He stops his car.

"You're kidding, right?"

"I just saw you and had to say hi," he says, somewhat sheepishly.

"Fuck off!"

"Whoa there, princess. That is a compliment. Why the hostility?"

She looks at him incredulously. "You stalking me in a parking lot is a compliment?"

"Yeah, babe, why don't you give me your number? We can grab drinks."

She looks at him and pulls out her phone. "Can I get a picture of you? I want to show my girlfriends how lucky I am that you stopped for me."

"Sure," he says.

She smiles, all charm, as she takes the picture and leans into his car.

"Show me."

"What?"

"Your cock, pull it out. I want to see it."

He looks around, wondering if this can be real. And he does as she asks. She takes another picture.

"Put that tiny thing away. Now here's what's going to happen: you will leave me alone, and you will never stalk a woman in a parking lot or anywhere. And never ever pull out your dick."

"You asked me to!"

"Listen, dude, if I was packing such a little thing, I wouldn't, but if some chick ever does date you, warn her you have a micro dick."

"Fucking bitch!"

"Yes, that's right, a bitch who has a picture of you, your car, and one micro penis. Cops love to see that kinda thing."

He frowns and drives off.

She gets in her car, thankful for being out of earshot of any more insanity the outside world has to offer. She wishes she could somehow find sanity in the world, but it's all just so mad with no end in sight.

She drives to work wishing she could be insulated from the moodiness and proclivities of the clients.

Why did I choose this?

Then she wondered if anything was an actual choice.

Does life just happen to us, or do we happen to it?

She is good at her job, well regarded and sought after for her services. She makes her own schedule; if she needs to take a day off, she can. She has no one to answer to. But she needs more. It seemed like her appetite is never satisfied.

Her friend had repeatedly told her, "One day you won't be as sought after, and you will regret being annoyed with all the desire." He meant it more for the catcalls, but she took it the same way. People, for the most part, annoyed her, which is one thing she liked about him, as he pretty much felt the same way.

He was a good friend.

Should it be more?

Before she realized it, she was parking outside her office. She hadn't even registered the ride.

twenty-three

he stares at the blank page on the desktop, as if somehow, magically, the computer was going to have answers to creative questions that he did not.

He sighs. This wasn't unusual. Getting stuck was often part of the deal, so he didn't worry. He put on some music, paced, and thought about the story. It usually got him a word, a spark, some trail to follow.

Sometimes, a word led to more words, then sentences, paragraphs and pages, and sometimes it led to nothing, less than nothing, other than the feeling that the creative dream was nothing but some bullshit he had sold himself. That he was a hack, or worse, a phony.

Saigon watches him as he dances around a bit to a song he likes and mutters to himself. The dog probably doesn't understand the creative process any better than he does, but as long as the food and butt scratchings keep coming, Saigon likely doesn't care.

He slides into his chair, head filled with words to make dance together on the page. Some days, the words dance better than others, but he is used to the battle and has made peace with it. The writing Gods are sometimes silent, or off doing something else, and too occupied to tell him what to write. He just trusts they would let him know what to put down. He is a conduit, not an artist, not a real creator. He just knows how to listen to the people who are not phonies like him.

Truth be told, he is a cathartic writer. This was the gift the writing Gods gave to him. Feel it all: pain, joy, sorrow, happiness. It was a blessing and a curse. The ability to have the setting of sensitivities, to *feel,* was incredible, yet at the same time, the weight of the world rested on his shoulders, just as it had on Atlas's.

He is writing about pain and sorrow. For some reason, that is easier for him than happiness and joy as a subject matter. Relaxing and enjoying life were challenges for him. Naturally, he wondered why, and all he could come up with was a fear and anxiety that if he truly enjoyed something, it would only be taken from him.

Life is sick, but only because of the sickness of those trying to live it.

Yet it is our afflictions and proclivities that make us interesting, vulnerable, jiggly balls of carbon matter.

He shrugged his shoulders. He didn't want to work. He wanted to fuck.

What's new?

He had been sticking to himself. With all the business with the ex haunting him, it was better that he stayed off women. It wouldn't last, this he knew. Saigon knew, the Writing Gods knew.

I am resigned to a life of monk-like masturbation.

Wait, do monks jerk off?

Kill me.

More pain, more sorrow, more dancing words upon a page. He rationalizes that he must fuck on to support his creativity.

Yes!!!!

Now if he can justify the excess weed, he will be in business.

Wait.

He is in a trancelike state, as if on autopilot, when his phone alerts him a text message has arrived. He finds himself finishing a sentence.

He had written two pages like a Sibyl in a prophetic trance at an oracle.

The text was from his friend, asking if the date was still okay for dinner. He responded immediately. Nothing was worse than an unanswered text.

Can you pick me up?

He hated driving, as he should, since he was awful at it. He had driven her once, on her birthday, when he had insisted she be taken out. He wondered if she noticed he was a shit driver, but even if she had, she would have never said.

She was taking him to a steakhouse, which made him feel bad. All overpriced meals that someone offered to pay for had the same effect. His trick was to eat before he went on such excursions so that he could claim he wasn't so hungry and just have an appetizer. It was silly, really. People who offered such celebratory meals would not have cared for the expense, yet the guilt remained. No matter what happened, we are always still stuck living with ourselves. No escape. Ever.

twenty-Four

she is on time, almost, which is pretty good. She knows how he preferred being prompt and doesn't want to make him wait.

Ten Minutes

She texts him her ETA.

She pulls into his driveway. It's a decent house, in a quiet neighborhood. Lots of woods surround it. She has been inside, but just once. They had shared margaritas on the porch, and he made a cheese and prosciutto plate that was memorable.

What was probably memorable for him was how she kept teasing him. She had worn a loose button-down shirt and no bra, often letting him get a glimpse of her breasts. She could see him looking without trying to be obvious. It hadn't really worked.

She doesn't know exactly why she had been so salacious. Perhaps she'd wanted to seduce him, not that that was so much of a challenge for her with anyone—it wasn't. She knows he's attracted to her, and she is pretty sure he knows she feels the same. What she doesn't know is what would ever happen beyond the friendship.

She texts him when she pulls into his driveway, and soon after he comes outside from a garage door opening. He smiles at her, and she returns the gesture as if it were all so very normal. It's not.

"Thanks for picking me up," he says, getting in the car. "You're a real gentleman."

She laughs and she pushes the button on her GPS. As she does, he looks at her curiously.

"What?" she asks.

"I thought you said it was one of your favorite restaurants?"

"It is."

"But you don't know how to get there?"

"Not really," she answers.

"I can tell you where to go. Take a left out of the driveway."

She starts to pull out to the right.

"Oh, I see," he says.

"See what?"

"You are directionally challenged. Take the other left."

"I thought you knew."

"You have never driven me before. How could I?"

"No?"

"No."

And with that, they listen to music and chat on the way to dinner, having no idea what was about to happen as a result.

The steakhouse is on the water. Although it is too cold to eat outside, they sit at a table with a view. They sit across from each other at first, but after ordering drinks and having a sip or two, he feels emboldened enough to sit next to her.

"What are you doing?" she asks him.

"Sitting next to you, of course."

"Who said you could do that?"

"Me."

"I see," she says, smiling.

She isn't against it. Although she isn't sure if she is for it either.

The food comes. He had wanted sushi rolls, which is an odd choice for a steakhouse, but he had ordered well and doesn't eat much. She gets him a piece of cake, which they share after the meal and several drinks.

During the meal, their fingers touch, brushing against each other perhaps innocently.

In the parking lot, he grabs her, pulling her toward him and kissing her.

They both feel the passion surge through them. Perhaps it's the tequila talking, or perhaps it's more. They finally break the embrace at her behest.

"People are watching," she says.

"Let them."

They get in the car, and she puts his address into the GPS. He sniggers.

"Be quiet or I won't take you home."

She drives very slowly, and he watches her concentrating on the road.

"I think you should maybe stay at my house. I have a spare room."

"Oh yeah," she chortled. "Why would I do that?"

"It's a long ride back to your place, and you're drunk."

"What makes you say that?"

"You never drive this slow."

They get to his house, and he shows her the spare room, but she joins him in his, under the pretense she will go to her room eventually. She never does.

twenty-five

she leaves the next morning. They didn't have intercourse, but they did have sex. He was surprised how much he liked having her there. His ex wasn't a fan of staying over, so it was a bit unusual for him.

He tries to make it feel normal. He takes Saigon for a walk in the woods. He goes to the gym. He writes. He can't stop thinking about her.

It's both horrible and wonderful at the same time. She has been in his life for years, but they were obviously moving in a new direction. Or were they?

Maybe not.

He texts her, thanking her for dinner.

You are welcome, I had a great time.

He thinks about asking her out, but it seems too soon. She wonders what he's doing. She had probed him, saying that he would only get back with his ex. He had assured her that he was done, that he had given it all he had and could give no more without accepting things would never change.

Life had its limits. Why shouldn't components of life have limitations too? It was like a ball of string: eventually the string, like the course of any relationship, ran out.

She hoped that he wouldn't go back, not because of her, but

for his own sake. She had watched him like a binge eater yo-yo back and forth, on again, off again. It was as if he were taking a drug he couldn't kick: carrying the shame of using, always saying it was the last time, only to go back again like the addict he was.

She knows she isn't one to talk. She was an addict herself. She doesn't judge him, at least not too much. She wants what is best for him, not for him to binge eat romantically.

She wonders what will happen next, but then she stops herself from such foolishness. She is considering dating again—well, not exactly. She does have a date for the weekend.

The guy she met on the Brooklyn Bridge had been texting with her, pushing, and asking, asking and pushing, for a date. Finally, she'd capitulated.

He isn't her usual type, then again, she wonders if she even has a type aside from wrong one.

Now she's having reservations, though. Should she go? She doesn't have any obligations to her friend, if that's what he still is. She had only taken him out for a birthday dinner. No, she will go on her date. The guy she had met was texting quite a bit, paying attention to her. He had even texted while they were at dinner the night before. Although, when he did, she had proclaimed how annoying he had been to do so. Her friend asked, and she just said something like "This person keeps texting me, I'm not sure why."

He had let it go as nothing remarkable, why would he think otherwise? She had barely mentioned it, besides her obvious aggravation to have to field the text during dinner in the first place. Although, he should perhaps have known better. She often spoke without context, as if she somehow believed that he possessed the one copy of the manual that was esoterically born when she was created.

A buddy calls and asks if he wants to meet for a drink or two. He agrees.

That's it, I'll ask her for a drink.

But he doesn't. He gets his act together to meet his friend, and one drink ends up being two joints and four drinks.

He wakes the next day, clothes strewn about his bedroom as if he had undressed himself in the middle of a hurricane. He spots a plate of food that contains melted cheese now laminated to the plate. Saigon seems content, lying on his back, legs in seven different directions, as if he had been the one abusing his liver.

He drags himself up and lets the dog out and feeds him. He's a good boy, not bothering his hungover master.

He wonders what she's doing. He wants to finish what he had started.

Busy today?

Working.

Meet for a drink after?

There's a strange pause. He had assumed it was a mutual feeling, the desire to see each other again, but the pause has him think he had miscalculated.

I have an errand but can meet you after. I work until two...

After? Now it was his turn to pause. What did that mean?

Text me.

It was Saturday. He wants to meet around four p.m., assuming that would be enough time for her errand.

He is wrong.

twenty-six

she didn't tell him about the date. She didn't think she needed to. She also thought about dipping on the date, but the guy was coming from Brooklyn, so she couldn't exactly stop it.

What does it matter, he will just go back to her . . .

At four, he decides to stop working. He's already showered, so he texts her.

Done working, off for a drink if you want to meet me.

The pause that follows makes him uneasy for some reason. She usually is quick to respond.

I don't think I will be available for a few hours.

Long errand.

Another pause, and he wonders what she's doing. He wonders what he's doing. He gets in his car and goes to a local spot that is average but has a good bar, sports on TV, and decent Italian. He could have a drink and a snack and go home if she didn't show. Her interest seems tepid at best.

I will text you when I am done, but I might be a bit.

He wonders what's going on in her mind. She was like him, brutally up front to a fault, yet this was mysterious. He is over-thinking, and he knows it, because that's what he did. Though he has no reason to do so; they messed around a little, no big deal.

Even if they had taken it further, there is no reason to believe it wouldn't be a one-off and back to business as usual.

He sits at the bar and orders. It's not packed, but also not empty. Two attractive women are to his right, and a guy entirely focused on his libation to his left. The rest of the joint is dotted with patrons here and there but not everywhere.

He sits there watching a soccer game, some European league. He wishes college football were on instead. His phone buzzes; it's her.

I didn't realize you were going out so early.

He doesn't respond right off. The guy next to him looks at him, his drink raised. He nods back at the guy.

Just HMU when you are done being so mysterious, see if I am still out and about.

She responds with a smiley face emoji.

"I hate soccer," the guy next to him says.

He laughs. "Must have a Euro crowd here or something."

"It *is* an Italian restaurant,"

"Right," he agrees.

"You alone?"

Is this guy hitting on me?

"For the mean time. I asked someone for a drink, but I'm thinking it's a no," he waves his hand across the empty stool.

"So just killing time?"

"And brain cells," he said, lifting his margarita.

"I am killing some myself. Can I join you?"

He wasn't in the habit of making new friends, but what was going to happen? He could leave, or maybe she would bail him out. Either way, he was there, trying to be present.

He nods, and the guy saddles up next to him.

"I appreciate your kindness," the stranger says.

"I've been accused of a lot of things, but . . ."

The man stops him. "No, you don't understand, I've been having a hard time. I'm from out west. I moved out here with my girl and just a series of shit circumstances derailed my life."

He's wondering if this is a scam. What's the angle?

"So now, I decided to get really fucked up, and forget for a day, I know it will be worse in the morning, when I wake up, if I wake up."

He looks at the guy. *If???*

"Listen, man, I'm just a writer, and aside from you meeting me at a bar, I'm no Hemingway."

"You're no . . . oh, don't you guys thrive on experience?"

"Sometimes," he says.

"Well, let this be an experience."

He wants to get out of the arrangement he unwittingly entered.

The guy must sense his trepidation. "We should go to the bathroom, order more drinks. They will be here when we get back."

The stranger asks the bartender for a drink refill for both, and he gets up. "Come on,"

He shrugs and goes with him, unsure, on one hand, why, but sort of certain on the other.

In the bathroom, the guy locks the door and lays out white powder on the counter.

"You do party?"

"Not in a while,"

"It's your world, but I thought I would offer." The guy does two huge lines and leaves some for him.

It's a dark road. One he has been down before. Once in a blue moon is fine, he justifies, and takes a line. One is enough. He is full of energy.

"Thanks,"

The stranger does the last bit, and they exit. Back at the bar, their drinks are waiting. He feels better. Of course, it's only false euphoria, but he still likes it. He looks at is phone. She had texted she would be an hour or two, maybe less. He shrugged.

"Is that the date?"

"I dunno what anything is to be honest."

"Random, chick? Dating apps?"

He laughs. "No, hardly random, I've been friends with her for years."

"Oh, so it's not a date?"

"I dunno what the fuck it is."

"I'm confused," the stranger says.

"Get in line. Enough about me. What's going on with you?"

The guy laughs. "It's funny, isn't it? Two strangers probably have an easier time disclosing their damage and pain to each other than long-time partners or friends."

"I guess nothing at stake. Why wasn't there disclosure by someone close? I get the feeling . . ."

"Yeah, good instincts," he says.

"I'm not Sherlock Holmes here. You mentioned the numbing and the girl and derailed."

"Huh, I guess I did," he says, lifting his drink.

"Thanks for the pick-me-up. It had been a while. But how did you know I wasn't a cop?"

The guy laughs. "You're kidding, right?"

"That obvious?"

"Kinda, what did you think? I wanted to suck your dick?"

"Kinda," he says, chuckling.

The guy laughs again. "Thanks, man, I needed this."

He nods, his phone buzzes. It's her. Whatever she's doing, she seems to have time to text.

Are you still out?

He holds up his finger to his newfound friend as he responds.

"Listen," he tells the guy, "if you want to talk about whatever, you can."

"I appreciate that, my friend. It's not good and I am lost. Of course, I am not doing myself any favors, but I needed to relax."

"No judgment, obviously."

"Obviously."

"We moved here from California. She had a job offer that was too good to be true, enough money to put a down payment on a house. I was just doing handiwork where I could get it there, which I figured I could do the same here, but then the job didn't work out, and we had already bought the house, and she got sick."

"Sick?"

"Cancer, she was riddled with it."

"Jesus, wait, 'was'?"

"She was fine, and within months, she was gone."

"Oh my God, I can't believe it."

"Live life while you can, my friend. It can be shorter than you think."

He sighs. The story struck him profoundly, even though he didn't know this guy from Adam.

"You have any weed?" the guy asks.

"That I do!"

The men go to his car, and he grabs his pen and hands it to the guy, who smokes it and passes it back.

"You can keep it. I have more at home."

"I'd like to give you the rest of what I have." He hands him the bag of white powder.

He takes it, not sure if he wants to have it—it's enough to stay fucked up for a while—but he takes it anyway since the guy is making a gesture, an exchange, and he can't disappoint him now. He doesn't appear he could handle anything else negative.

I'm free, if you are still out, I can meet you.

"That looks like my cue," the guy says.

"I guess she is meeting me after all."

The guy hands him a card. "My number, I'd like to hear what happens."

He nods. "Sure, you okay to drive?"

"Yeah, the blow levels me out. It's not that far anyway. Thanks for this," he says, lifting the weed pen.

He extends his hand, but the guy comes in for a hug. It is awkward for him, but heartfelt at the same time. They break the embrace, and he watches the guy get into his beat-up black Toyota. He expects him to wave or something, but he does not. The guy drives away, like he wasn't there at all, and they hadn't just had a bonding moment.

He fingers the bag of cocaine, which was the only evidence that the guy had been there, telling his fucked-up story, drowning his pain in cocktails and illicit drugs. He goes back inside, orders another drink, and texts her back. He tells her where he is, and she responds quickly that she is on her way. She has no way of knowing that a stranger had kept him out. Had it not been for the random encounter, he would have had his drink and been tired of being out alone.

He goes to the bathroom and does another bump before returning to his post at the bar. He finds himself watching the door, attentive to her arrival, and when that moment comes, he stands, takes her coat, and pulls out her chair. She kisses him on the cheek, and he vaguely returns the benign gesture.

She looks good. She is wearing a jumper, which is unusual. He usually saw her in clothing that hugged her body.

"Can I order you a spicy margarita?"

"How did you know?"

"You always order them."

She smiles. *The devil is in the details.*

They sit and they drink, and they speak as they always have, but it isn't the same either. They touch and flirt in ways that are new and improved.

"You were so strange today," he states suddenly.

"I was?"

"I mean, I dunno, your 'errand' was so mysterious."

She bows her head a little bit, and then says, "Look, I didn't mean to be weird, but I didn't know how to deal with it."

"Deal with what?"

"I was on a date."

"Ah."

"Are you mad?"

"You could have told me; it isn't like you owe me anything."

"I almost didn't go. I mean, I didn't want to, but you didn't ask me out until this morning, I . . ."

"It's okay."

"As soon as I went, I regretted it, I was texting you the whole time."

"You really feel bad about it, I get it, like I said, you don't owe me anything."

"I tried to tell you at dinner the other night," she says.

"You did?"

"I guess not a good job of it, to be honest, I don't know what I'm doing."

"Can we forget about it? You are here now. That's what matters."

"Thanks for letting me off easy. I felt like an asshole."

"I'm sure you can find some way to make it up to me."

"Oh yeah?" she says.

"What do you say we get out of here?"

She looks at him for a moment, all the while knowing what she was going to say, but she makes him wait for her response anyway. Not that it mattered; he was pretty sure he knew how she would respond.

twenty-seven

they lay next to each other, separated slightly by Saigon, who apparently found comfort nestled between two humans, or perhaps needs to let her know that she has to compete for his time.

Her hand is draped across his body, as if it were almost his own appendage. When he woke, it freaked him out that there was not only a hand on him, skin on skin, but an entirely whole human being was there, too.

He gets up slowly, trying not to wake her, gently slipping her arm off him and onto the bed. He looks at her there, soft features relaxed into the warm hug of sleep. She is more beautiful to him in that moment than any other before. Sure, he had noticed she was pretty before, but he is seeing her through a different lens, and it floods him with feelings he didn't know he possessed.

Saigon gets up with his master, and she doesn't move, just rests there. He lets the dog out and makes coffee and brings two mugs in. She was so quiet as she slept, he feels a pang of guilt as she opens her eyes softly.

"I didn't mean to wake you."

She smiles as she stretches. "Is that coffee?"

"Yes, it is, just milk, right?"

"You remembered!"

"It was only a few days ago."

He hands her the mug, and she sits up and sips at it. He looks at her breasts as they sway gently as she moves. He catches himself staring at her and quickly moves to the other side of the bed to drink his own coffee.

They sit awkwardly for a moment. Finally he puts down the mug and moves to kiss her. She pulls away.

"I haven't brushed my teeth!"

"I don't care," he says.

The gesture is sweet, but too soon. She gets up and moves to the bathroom. He watches her go. He likes seeing her naked. After all the years he has known her, he hadn't realized he would enjoy the sight that much.

He gets up so that he can watch some more. She is at the second bathroom sink, which had been rendered useless until she had stayed the night a few days back. He had given her a toothbrush of her own and left it, in case she stayed again. He caught himself smiling at the notion that she had.

"What?" she asks, conscious of his gaze.

"Sorry, I don't mean to stare."

"Then stop," she says, sly grin included.

He laughs and returned to his coffee in bed, where she soon joins him, and they resume their physical activities from the previous evening.

She left a few hours later. They didn't say what would happen next, perhaps because they didn't know. What was clear was that things had changed for their relationship, and obviously it was an upgrade for both.

He looks at Saigon, who is stretched back out on the bed, happy his master's guest has stopped taking up space designated for him.

"Come on, Sai, let's go for a walk,"

The dog perks up and gets off the bed almost before the last word is uttered.

Out in the woods, he lets the dog off leash. Saigon leaps and bounds ahead. He likes that the dog can feel free, but he feels a degree of anxiety, too, that he will take off into the woods after a creature of some sort to hunt. His anxiety often gets the better of him; the overthinking is a mindfuck and then some. Self-imposed, no less!

Saigon doesn't go far enough to trigger the anxiety of losing his ever-present companion, but that doesn't mitigate overthinking and anxiety of other natures.

He realizes that his anxiety is always about loss. He doesn't want anything in which he can't control the narrative. Why would he? Eventually, if he loved something or someone, he would lose them somehow.

He thinks about her. He is having fun again. It has been a while since he enjoyed someone's company. He has enjoyed hers before, too, but romance changed the game. He has pushed all his chips into the middle of the table.

All in.

Was he, though?

The walk proves to be serene. He does overthink, but the dog doesn't wander off and she texts him half a dozen times. No one is abandoning him, at least not this day. It should be a relief, but it isn't, not exactly, not at all. Sometimes, there is nothing worse than getting exactly what one wants.

twenty-eight

they sit outside the Louvre at the cafe. They had two glasses of a deep, red wine and a cheese plate in front of them, untouched as always. They sit there as people pass them by, unable to take notice that they weren't doing anything of note, as if they were merely attractive ornaments on the tree of life.

"So, it has begun," she says without words.

"Are you not pleased?"

"It will never work."

"It won't?"

"It never does, does it?"

"Then what is the point of our little exercise?"

"To amuse us, no?"

He furrows his brow in a rare moment of emotionality for either creature.

"I just think we deserve some fun. Why not see what happens?" she proclaims.

"It's a bad mix. I am having regrets."

"Bad mix? It's all a bad mix, it all ends the same way, in pain."

"That's not entirely true," he points out.

"How so?"

"Death, there is no pain in that end."

"There is. You are being daft. The pain is for the ones left living."

He couldn't argue. She was right, of course. He sighed and absently picked up his wine and swirled the glass in hand before putting it back down.

"This is the fun part; we should enjoy it."

"You have always been smarter than me," he admits.

She smiles coquettishly, uncertain if he means it or not, but appreciating the idea.

"So, you want to call off our little game?" she asks.

He sits and thinks, shutting off the tornado of thoughts so that she cannot hear. She watches him intently; he sees her eyes on him and wonders if she can hear him despite his efforts to quiet himself to her consumption.

"Of course not. What would we do with ourselves?"

"We would waste away into nothingness, just like they do."

They both grimace internally, but they can each see the disdain of the other's thoughts.

"Back to the business at hand, then?" he asks.

"Indeed. Let's turn up the heat, shall we?"

"What do you have in mind?"

"I want to raise the stakes, naturally," she admits.

"I hate to ask what you are up to."

A slick smile dances across her face. He knows her too well, of course.

"I want them dripping in each other—gimme, gimme, gimme." Her voice in his head is almost lyrical.

"As you wish, but I fear for them. If you ratchet up everything, there is a deeper abyss to fall into."

She looks profoundly at him, and their obsidian eyes lock. He leans forward into her waiting arms. Her touch, although exceedingly rare, gives him chills, even after all this time and space that has passed between them.

"Trust that the journey is one we need to experience," she says, comforting him.

He melts into her further. She understands. She always has, and she always will.

twenty-nine

he asks her out on a date. Not a drink, not a hookup, he asks her to dinner.

She accepts. The guy she went out with keeps texting her, but she ignores him, thinking he will go away on his own, and when he persists, she shuts him down. She doesn't want to be mean, but she wants not to be annoyed.

He has asked her way in advance, and she has time to think about it. Before, he asked her for a drink the same day, so this was different.

Is it a date?

It feels like one, although she is venturing into new territory. They were friends, but now they have added sex. She assures herself it was just for some fun, that the sex will eventually ruin the friendship. She has nothing to lose, other than the friendship, but she figures after a while maybe, just maybe, they could resume it without too much consequence. She was mad at herself for overstepping an obvious boundary, yet at the same time, thrilled that she had.

It was nothing new; she'd always enjoyed his company. And she had contemplated the match before when her overcalculating mind did the math. It came out well each time she did the calculus.

Don't think, just enjoy.

But she did think. She likes these thoughts, and she knows her emotions will get the better of her if she allows it. The problem is that she doesn't have control. This is who she is, and this is how it is going to be.

She thinks of what she will wear and decides she should probably go shopping for something new. She laughs as she catches herself overdoing it.

Why not?

She looks online on her phone as she drives to work, knowing that she won't have time to do so between clients. She could talk to them; some know about her friend but don't know the salacious detail that they had graduated to lovers.

She almost gets into an accident looking at potential date outfits while driving. She puts the phone down, not being able to afford the jitteriness that comes with being online while operating a motor vehicle. She had a few days to put together an ensemble anyway.

Her phone pings, just as she had made peace not to text and drive. She looks at the phone in the well, and then back to the road. It is trying to suck her into something she has already acknowledged she shouldn't be doing.

Maybe it's him. . . .

Her eyes oscillate between phone and road as if she is watching a tennis match. She growls at the phone, as if it will understand the promise she has made to herself. The phone pings again.

"Fuck off!!"

But the phone doesn't fuck off. Someone is texting her, and persistently so.

There is a bit more tennis, another growl, until finally she capitulates.

"Are you kidding me?"

She tosses the phone back into the well; it isn't a pleasant toss by any standard.

When she gets to work and finally parks, she picks up the phone. She reads the text again from the suitor she never should have gone out with in the first place. She is beyond annoyed—not only is the guy she doesn't want texting her sending her texts, but the one she wants to text her isn't. She begins composing an angry text telling the guy she isn't interested and to fuck off, but she catches herself and instead does the humane thing and blocks him and deletes his contact.

Good morning.

She texts to get some of the digital attention she wants. She sits in the car waiting a moment, dressing herself in her mind for the dinner, and not admitting she is waiting for him to brighten her day. She sighs when she isn't instantly gratified, finally opting to get out of her car and go to work.

thirty

in the gym, Insta-chick is filming herself again. He is annoyed by the superficiality of it. She stops to wave at him, and he regrettably feigns a smile, inadvertently inviting her over.

"Hey!"

He has his earbuds in, and even though it isn't so complicated to understand what she has said, he points and pulls one out of his ear.

"Sorry, the music is loud."

"I haven't seen you in a bit. We don't hang out anymore," she says.

"Oh, I've been busy. In fact, I am in a rush. Can we connect another time?"

"Yeah? I'd like that," she responds, touching his arm.

For fuck's sake.

He fakes another smile and puts in his earbud, not noticing that she keeps looking over at him. What he does notice is a text from her. It is a simple "good morning," but he likes knowing she has thought of him. He doesn't answer right off. He wants to get out of the gym as unscathed as possible.

He runs to the Starbucks around the corner for some much-needed non-narcotic stimulant, and while he waits for his order to be fulfilled, he texts her back, catching himself watching the sex they had in his mind's eye, as if he is some sort of third person in a voyeuristic pose. When he comes out of his haze, his name is being called by the barista to fetch his drink. When he steps up to retrieve it, the person who hands him the beverage asks him what's so amusing. He scoffs, but as he turns, he understands that the imagery that has just danced through his head has actually made him happy.

You are fucked.

He would like to be fucked, but in the fun sense, not in the proverbial one. He could go back to the gym, knowing full well Intsta-chick will do whatever, but that isn't the fucking he is after. He shakes his head at the realization.

FUCKED.

thirty-one

she picks him up for their dinner. When he gets into the car, he kisses her painted lips lightly, and they are off. They chitchat with a certain ease and comfortability that would be expected from good friends, except now it is enhanced—more engagement to match, more at stake. He lays a hand on her leg while she drives. Now that he has touched her, he is having issues not touching her. She tries to pretend it is all quite casual, as if nothing is happening, that his hand isn't on her leg, that she doesn't want him to move it. Finally, rather than buck it, she moves her hand over his, and their fingers interlace like pieces of a puzzle that have been connected before.

At the restaurant, they seat him in the corner table he requests, and they shake his hand and acknowledge him by name. He asks if he may order her a cocktail, and she smiles and agrees. He asks a series of questions designed to make sure she is comfortable with the meal choices he now feels emboldened to make.

They touch often in the euphoria a new couple is wont to do. He is very affectionate toward her, more than she is used to or typically enjoys in a public setting. She knows many people in and around the area, and she doesn't want unnecessary gossip, even if it is of a positive nature.

They are fully engaged with each other. It is powerful, intense, and grows more with each drink they have. The food doesn't mitigate the swoon, partially because it isn't entirely fueled by libation.

The restaurant is full, but to them, no one else registers. The waiter even isn't even acknowledged, except when they want to leave, which they do expeditiously. The meal has been a formality to the main course of ravaging each other.

Both express themselves best physically, and once united in such an embrace, it seems impossible to not be. Euphoria is afoot, and no one complains.

The night, middle of the night, early morning, and morning are filled with more of the same. In between, they are still, but remain focused on each other, staring into each other's eyes, as if their souls were intertwined in some secret dance.

"I'd like to take you to a spot I like," she says, breaking the silence.

"Oh?"

"Yeah, I mean, you took me to one of your spots . . ."

"It wasn't done with the expectation you have to reciprocate."

"No, I didn't take it as such."

He shrugs. "Sure, show me what you got."

"Saturday?"

He nods and gets out of bed, catches her watching him sway about as he leaves the room, and doesn't wait long so she can also observe the return trip. He is carrying a fluffy towel.

"In case you want to shower," he says, aware of her eyes.

"You are really full service!"

"I try."

She gets up and now it's his turn to watch. He slaps her ass playfully as she walks by, taking the towel. She disappears into the shower, and he realizes he is smiling.

Saigon lies on the floor, his spot in the bed usurped by his master's guest. He is unaccustomed to this, as his master isn't into being a host.

He slips on some shorts. "Sorry, bud, let's get you outside."

The dog follows him out and he opens the door for him. He leaves it open while he makes Saigon's breakfast. He trots in, expecting his meal, his routine not thrown off by not having his typical accommodations in bed next to his master.

He pours two mugs of coffee and brings them into the bedroom. He finds her towel-wrapped, back in bed, almost waiting for this delivery.

She smiles as he hands her the mug. She looks inside and sees that he has made it the way she likes, despite only saying it once.

Two nights, morning coffee the way I like. It will never last.

She sips her coffee slowly, as if the sands of an hourglass control how long she can stay.

"So, what's the place you want to show me?" he asks.

"You don't trust me?"

Is it a test?

"Of course, I'm sure if you like it, I will, too."

"I will pick you up at six thirty or seven-ish, okay?"

He nods, and as he does, she puts her mug of hourglass sand down and gets dressed. He watches her as she does, not wanting to give away that he doesn't want her to leave. Still, the promise of more time has been made, and after she is in her previous night's clothes, he puts on a shirt and walks her to her car. They kiss.

"Saturday?" he says, breaking the embrace.

"Saturday."

Saturday.

thirty-two

he moves about the room with music blaring, hoping to encourage the words he needs on a page out from hiding. It isn't working. He is more involved in his newfound romance—and he isn't even certain that is what it is.

Saigon frolics about with a rope toy, unaware of his master's dilemma. He watches the dog, envious of him briefly, before sitting down at his desk in a futile effort.

Finally, he looks to Saigon, and the dog looks at him.

"Want to go for a hike?"

Saigon cocks his head before jumping on his master for further approval.

"Okay, let's go."

Out in the woods, he meditates on his unwritten story, all the while distracted with the other story being written.

Saigon is in lockstep with him, as if he knows he needs the moral support on both creative and romantic endeavors.

They stop at a stream, and the dog sniffs briefly at a frog, who is unmoved that a dog has paid him any notice.

He watches the stream, as if, in some Zen moment, he is realizing the meaning of life.

"That's it, come Sai, before my thought blows away."

His companion follows him back out the way they came. They hop in the car and drive home, where he sits and makes the words dance. He is thrilled with a five-page output and the fact that he has left off in a spot where he knows how to continue once he is ready to work again.

He smokes a celebratory joint and returns a text from her, confirming the date she has suggested.

It was a rare moment of success on multiple fronts. He cared for her, but the recentness of his previous failure made him pump the brakes. It was fun, he rationalized.

Just enjoy the ride.

He giggled immaturely, as he was susceptible to do on occasion. It was easier to express himself physically. There was no danger in friends with benefits. Romance, that was perilous. He knew that firsthand, but most did. He didn't want to be alone, but simultaneously, the thought of being with people for prolonged amounts of time was not an alluring prospect either. It had to be different for him choosing a romantic partner. She had to be more tolerable, and even then, he would, in all likelihood, find ways to sabotage them unconsciously. He was, like most members of the species, flawed and fucked up. In all fairness, he tried to be better, as chasing off people who wanted to be around him would inevitably leave him bereft of human contact, not that it was the worst concept he could think of. Yet, when he succeeded in such plots against himself, he engaged in some sort of act of self-hatred.

He found himself thinking about her more than he liked. It was lack of control that filled him with disdain. But on the flip side, he was seeing a part of her he had only heard about second hand, and now that their friendship had added attributes, he was privy to such things and then some. That, he was okay with.

They texted daily now, basically all day. She was feeling very girlfriendy, despite having not discussed such exclusivity. He wasn't talking to anyone else but wasn't sure he was ready for that leap into committed status either. He didn't know exactly what he wanted, other than for this, whatever it was, to continue.

For some reason, he thought of some of the escapades she had told him about, and now it bothered him.

No, that's not right, why?

He blames the weed; he is overthinking. He does so sober and more so during libation-influenced situations. He decides to have a beer in hopes his stoned mind will calm down. Saigon is already in bed, sprawled over all the pillows, roughing it.

"Come on, dude."

The dog lifts his head in the hopes a vague acknowledgment will do the trick and get his master off his back. It does not. He pushes him gently, and Saigon begrudgingly moves, allowing him to share the bed with his princely canine.

He flips on the TV, finds some sports, and reads at the same time. He has his phone with him just in case she texts him. He is mildly annoyed at this, as it is new and has everything to do with her. He had previously taken vacations from his phone, especially when at home decompressing, and now he found himself checking it, annoyed at nothing to report, or receiving something from someone other than her.

She texts him often, she says nice things, and he says nice things in return. It is a change of pace for him, and he wonders why he hadn't had this discovery with her sooner. There is a substance, a depth, that is beyond the novelty. Despite there being no complaints, he craves the understanding of something he will not likely ever understand. Sometimes, perhaps, one should simply enjoy the ride before any crash.

thirty-three

she finds herself texting him often, almost like a boyfriend. He is not a boyfriend, and from what she thinks of him, she wonders if he could play that role in her movie.

She also knew him well enough; she kept thinking he would go back to his ex. He said he had reached his boiling point and that this time was different. She had heard it before, and maybe she didn't want to sell herself a dream.

Fun, this was fun. She didn't know why she had to reassure herself of the endeavor's nothingness. Perhaps it was a bit of self-preservation. This was new. Normally she dove in headfirst, with reckless abandon, but this was somehow different.

Proceed with caution.

She didn't know what she was doing. Then again, she was a "fly by the seat of her pants" kind of gal, at least romantically speaking. Of course, she was well aware of his history, as he was expertly versed in hers.

He knows where the bodies are buried.

This, for all intents and purposes, should have provided a modicum of relief. It does not. Instead, it causes a plethora of anxiety. She is being wholly irrational, of course. He knew her and cared about her regardless of what he knew. The irrationality was born from her own judgment of his past, but it didn't stop her from wanting to see where all this would land, not that she thinks it would.

He was a serial, not always so, monogamist. She knew of hedonistic desires that had been acted out in other situations. She wondered, of course, if the same would be required of her. She wasn't sure if she was up for the task.

Overthinking.

She wants not to have him on her mind but finds that she can't help it. She wants answers that she can't have, no matter how badly she wants them. She is driving a thousand miles an hour in a ten-mile-an-hour lane. This is her curse. As with most curses, it had its share of benefits as well, although she couldn't necessarily figure out what those were. It didn't matter. She is who she is, and that will not change. It never did.

Still overthinking.

She just can't help herself; things are good, too good. She fights against enjoying what is happening. On occasion, she is able to talk herself down, but she already cares about him, and now those feelings are on steroids.

Don't overthink! This is good, this is fun.

She gets into her car, not realizing that her shirt is on inside out and backward.

The drive to work in the morning always feels arduous, always traffic, always assholes driving too fast or too slow. She does things one shouldn't while driving: text, shop for clothes or shoes she most likely would just end up returning.

Finally, she texts him, asking if he has time for a call. This was a progression, something more personal, voice contact, in a digital communication world that they had lived in mostly.

They chitchat as they had when they were just friends, but there is added excitement that neither is detecting but is most certainly there. It all seems quite natural, at least to them.

They discuss their upcoming plans, and each says that they are looking forward to it. She tells him about the spot—it's ethnic, a taste of her heritage. It was nothing he had ever tried, but he was adventurous, he would love to try anything she introduced.

The call ends, both smiling not so secretly, except maybe from themselves.

thirty-four

they sit in what looks like impossibly comfortable clothes, incredibly relaxed, but what they are is bored. Their boredom not only dampens their level of apparent comfort, but it also eradicates it.

They are in the gardens of Versailles, a secret nook where no one can see them, even if some random people came by, they wouldn't be able to see these beings. They are there, but also, they are not.

Still, they sit next to each other on a bench made of stone. No one comes into their little enclave, and they are there for some time, seemingly staring at a wall of shrubs such that if you saw them there, it may look to you like they were at a sports bar, rapt, watching a game. They are just being their usual selves. Sitting and communicating without words.

"This isn't as interesting as I had hoped," she says, matter of fact.

"I understand, but what did you expect?"

"I'm not sure, more of something . . ."

"Give it time. Something always goes south, it always does."

Her face moves, one may even call it a smile of some sort. Regardless, the idea of failure seems much more appealing than success. Success is what is supposed to happen, par for the course. It's when we fall flat on our faces that things get interesting.

"Perhaps we should nudge the situation," she suggests.

"You are truly insatiable!"

She crosses her legs, uncrosses them, and then crosses again in opposite direction.

His eyes shift at her in one last bastion of what's left of his humanness.

"I am what I am. You are well aware of my appetites."

"Yes, I suppose I am. What more do you want?"

"A bit of doom would be a nice start."

"You have something in mind?" he asks.

"You pick, but please don't disappoint me."

"I would never. How can you even suggest such a thing?"

She sighs.

thirty-five

the day goes slowly for him. He cannot concentrate, as he has her on his mind. Relentless text exchanges, with a side order of speaking once or twice on the phone—whatever is happening, it has intensified a thousand-fold.

The physical aspect has intensified, as well: affection and sexuality are both intense and frequent when they are together. Together ends up being two days a week. It is unclear to either of them how that became the norm.

She finds herself wanting more, but this, whatever it is, has been going on for only a month, and she can't say anything . . . yet. She also is paranoid that she is just a rebound, and she is aware how saying something may portend. Silence is golden, for now. She was on the fence about what was happening; it was her first encounter taking a solid friendship to the next level, but she is comfortable, and she is happy. He treats her like a lady in the ways she wants, and not like one also the ways she wants. It makes her a bit nervous that he is checking so many boxes, but she manages to talk herself down.

Just enjoy it.

He is curious about where she is taking him and looks up the spot online. The menu is foreign to him despite the fact he is a self-proclaimed foodie. He doesn't recognize much. He is looking forward to the meeting but certainly not because of the food.

He sits looking at Saigon, who is napping with enthusiasm.

"How can you be so calm?"

The dog lifts his head vaguely as if to ask, "Did you say something?" but when his master fails to expound, he resumes his nap.

"Fine."

He looks in his closet, pulling out pants to see if they are clean, and he discovers a stain here and a stain there. He grunts in frustration as he tosses the pants on the ground. Saigon leaps off the bed and sniffs at the pile of pants. He then plops down on the pile unceremoniously. His master looks at him incredulously.

"And I wonder why . . ."

Saigon doesn't wonder. He just makes himself more comfortable, even as another pair of pants is flung over him, followed by some shirts.

Finally, he comes to a reasonably matching, clean ensemble for his night out. He hangs the curated outfit in the bathroom, praying that it's safe. He stops to look at himself in the mirror, realizing that his effort is beyond casual.

For fuck's sake!

He watches as the reflection shakes its head, in part disapproval, part incredulousness. Granted, he liked to look good, but preselecting outfits?

I have gone mad, for sure.

He takes a deep breath. He has hours before they see each other, so he drapes the preordained outfit over a chair and lies on the bed. Saigon seems to agree with the idea and joins him.

He turns on the television, grateful for college football. He has found that he keeps his phone next to him, in case she texts, which she does, often. He is restless, and he knows it. Perhaps it is the anticipation. Truth be told, he has no idea what he is doing. He had built in care for her already, and now things have intensified. It is confusing, to be sure. The feelings are there, and what he is currently experiencing and the relationship he had just got out of were night and day.

This wasn't the first time he had jumped from one thing to another. It was odd. The last time was unexpected, just as this was. Yet perhaps it was no accident. Why, at times like these, did we wonder if there were invisible forces at work?

Why would someone appear in your life like that if one wasn't ready to accept them?

Of course, there was no answer to this, or most things. Apparently, we all just wander about and haven't a clue as to what we are doing, not really. He supposed there was a certain charm to this foible of humanity, at least that is what he chooses to tell himself.

Despite having a remedial understanding as to what was going on, he remained confused. It was a conflict of sorts. This person, his friend now turned lover, this person with whom he laughed with and enjoyed her company, had arrived at an inopportune moment. Or was it the perfect one? Regardless, she had arrived, and they were engaged to a degree, but deep down, he knew that degree would have to increase, or he may not only lose his companion, but also his longtime friend.

Was it the risk that made it so alluring?

She had a track record of getting tired of people and worldly possessions, often sending them on their way without a second thought. It never occurred to him before, but he could also end up in the unwanted pile.

At this point, he wasn't sure what pile he was in: wanted or soon to be unwanted. He was overthinking and he knew it.

Enjoy. Enjoy. Enjoy.

thirty-six

i'm here.

He sees her text.

I'm coming.

He makes a last-minute check in the mirror. He should be relieved to be taking the final once-over after making copious amounts prior, not that it registered. He is wrapped up in her spell, and he is a little stoned.

He takes a piece of gum, also superfluous since he is already chewing some. He gives Saigon a treat, and the dog takes it gleefully, suddenly not caring that his master is leaving him. He chuckles at the notion that creatures of all types become distracted by something.

He walks out to her car and gets in the passenger seat.

"Hi," she says.

"Hi," he repeats.

He moves in for a kiss, letting her dictate the lightness of it. Since she is wearing her trademark red lipstick, she allows her lips to dust his.

"Sorry, I should have held off on painting my lips."

"It's okay, we can make up for it later."

She smiles.

He smiles.

"I hope you like this place," she says.

"I like trying new things. I am excited."

"Good," she says, pulling out of his driveway and into the night.

"What is this music?"

"Miley Cyrus, I think."

"It's good,"

They drive on the dark country roads, music playing, wondering what the other is thinking.

"So, they have a kind of dumpling, if you like that sort of thing," she says, breaking the silence.

"I am in your hands. Show me the way to your cultural cuisine. I'm a good eater and will try almost anything."

"Shit," she says.

"What's the matter?"

"I think we're lost."

"I thought you have been here before?" he asks.

"As if that matters. I have a terrible sense of direction."

"Okay, well you are using GPS."

"Just doesn't seem right."

He starts to say something but then thinks better of it. And as it turns out, he doesn't have to, as they emerge from the darkness into a small swath of town.

"Must be here somewhere, no?"

"I think so?"

"When was the last time you were here?"

"I dunno, maybe summer, it was light out."

He looks at the well-lit street and chuckles.

"What?" she asks.

He looks at her and just smiles. "You're cute, that's all."

"There it is!" she says, pointing excitedly.

They park, get out of the car, and walk to the restaurant. Inside, it is unassuming: a basic bar and nothing from the decor would indicate that this was an Eastern European restaurant. It is utterly nondescript.

The restaurant is devoid of customers, which is a bit discouraging for her and concerning for him.

"I guess I didn't need to make a reservation," she says, dejectedly.

They stand unattended. There is no one tending the bar, and no one has come out to seat them.

"Hello?" he offers finally.

A woman enters hurriedly from the back. She speaks to the woman in her language, and the woman responds by offering a wave of the hand to the tables that are all sadly available.

"She says we can sit wherever we want."

He nods. "I was getting that. How about there?"

She looks at the corner table that he has suggested and nods. They walk over, and he takes her coat and then his own.

"It was busier the last time I was here," she admits.

"It's not an issue. I came here for your company, not to see other assholes I don't even know. Besides, if the food isn't good, we can just have at it on the table. No one will care."

"Ha! The way we go at it, I think we would have to charge for the show."

He smiles. The sex is good. It's very good. They hadn't verbalized it; they really didn't need to. They just sort of resumed business as usual, except the business between them had obviously changed. He thought about it as she sat looking at the menu, carefully explaining to him what each dish was as she considered it.

It was important to her that he was happy. When she looks up from the menu, she catches him watching her, a Cheshire cat style grin on his face, as he doesn't appear shy about being caught staring.

He was the one who usually ordered. She liked the dynamic, and it worked out well for both. This night is obviously different, sort of. She still lets him choose after an explanation of what their choices are.

They laugh at how empty the restaurant is.

"Do I dare order a cocktail?" she asks him.

"Wine seems like a safe bet," he responds.

"I don't know these wines," she says, handing him the menu.

He looks at it and shrugs. "I guess ask what is similar to Pinot Grigio. That's the go-to, right?"

She smiles and nods, thrilled that he knows her patterns. Most men didn't pay attention to her specific needs, or anyone's needs other than their own. He was different, he always had been, and she had thought this before. She wondered if it occurred to him too, or if she was just a plaything whenever he got bored. Yet he seemed engaged, at least to a degree. When they were together, especially the last few weeks, since things had taken a physical turn, things were very, very intense.

He chuckles after they order, as she had still managed to get him to choose, despite it being her culture and choice of restaurant.

"Do you think they are making the wine in the back," she asks, empty-handed.

"Probably, I saw them stomping on some grapes earlier."

They laugh, and he reaches across the table and touches her hand. It is a small connection in the physical sense, but it carries an electric, emotional charge that packs a punch.

The wine finally arrives. They must have thought it belonged with the food, as it all comes at once.

"I hope you like it," she says.

"Looks good. How's the wine?"

She slides the glass to him. He sips at it, and his cringe betrays him.

"That's how I felt about it."

"Let's try the food," he suggests.

There are two types of large dumplings and a stew of some sort. She serves him a dumpling from each steaming bowl.

"You grab them here," she says, demonstrating.

"Like this?" he says, grabbing the food not so smoothly, almost dropping it.

"One is cheese, one is meat, no clue which is which."

She nods at him to try it, and he does. When he bites into it, hot juice squirts out the opposite site, burning his hand slightly.

"Shit!" he says quickly, putting down the rest of the dumpling.

"Shit!" she echoes, seeing what has happened.

She rescues his doused shirt with her napkin dipped in water.

"I should have warned you they do that."

"Thank you," he says, noting her care.

She was caring. She always had been. He wondered why he hadn't noticed it until now. Perhaps it was his limited exposure to her as a friend. He realized that when she took him out to dinner for his belated birthday, without that, the moment he was currently experiencing wouldn't even exist.

"That was the meat. The cheese should be less squirtish," she says.

He laughs at her play on language, unsure if he should correct her, or if she is indeed speaking a language all her own. Either way, he is amused, does as instructed, and tries the cheese version.

"I think I like the cheese one better; it doesn't attack you while you eat."

She laughs.

They eat and laugh some more. They have the entire place to themselves. Not that it mattered, for even had the restaurant been full, they still would have had the space they occupied to themselves.

thirty-seven

she doesn't want to get out of bed. They slept very little, and she wants to resume the non-sleeping activities. But she can't stay. She has family obligations.

He gets up out of bed slowly. Saigon, it seems, has been staring at him, giving his master the cue to take him out and feed him.

"Where are you going?" she asks.

"Let the dog out. I will bring coffee if you have time."

"Is it okay if I hop in the shower?"

"Let me get you a towel," he says, disappearing briefly.

He comes back with a towel, which he places in the bathroom. He notices that he feels uncharacteristically comfortable with her in his space, so much so that he was being a poor host, not doing a good job assuring her comfort. This wasn't a surprise for her, as she had been close to him and knew that he didn't have people over so often. Until recently, she hadn't been in his space herself.

In the shower, she thinks how nice this is. Then the pessimist who lives inside her tells her how it all will go to shit. It always does.

He will cheat.

He will get back with his ex.

He will move away.

He will never love me.

She leaves the comfort of the warm shower, wondering how many other women have done this same routine. But she forgets it when she sees a steaming cup of coffee waiting for her on the bathroom counter. She sips at it, savoring its perfect flavor, made exactly how she likes.

Little things.

She walks out of the bathroom, naked and expecting him to be there, but he is not. She lays down on the bed, thinking he will come back, but when it becomes apparent that he won't, she looks at the clock.

Late.

She gets dressed and is greeted by Saigon as she leaves the bedroom and makes her way to the kitchen.

"Babe?"

Shit.

She is a bit alarmed that she called him that.

"Coming," he says from his office.

He enters harried and, seeing she is leaving, experiences a sinking feeling he wasn't prepared for.

"What's the matter?"

"Sorry, I have a morning routine. I'm not used to overnight guests."

"Oh, I didn't mean to disrupt your day," she says, feeling awkward. Or was it her own reason to bolt guilt-free?

He pulls her close to him and holds her. This is more needy than he is okay with feeling.

"I had a good time. Thank you for showing me something new."

"I always have a good time with you, even before, when we were just friends," she admits, surprising herself.

They break the embrace.

"I will walk you down," he says.

"You don't have to."

"I want to."

He opens the door to his basement and down the stairs they go, neither admitting the dread they both feel at parting. She betrays herself a bit in her kiss. It is hungry, and he feels it. Finally, they break the embrace, and she gets into her car. He opens the garage for her, and she leaves.

They wave but say nothing.

She backs out, waves again, and is gone.

They have said nothing about seeing each other again. She wonders if that is it.

Why wouldn't he say something?

She drives home absently, overthinking as she does.

Back inside the house, he does his share of overthinking, as well. Saigon greets him, as though he hasn't seen him in years.

"Geez, dude."

The dog acts as if he has been neglected forever. Granted, she distracted him a little—no, no, it was a lot, but still.

"All right, I will make it up to you. Wanna go for a walk?"

Saigon cocks his head in obvious interest.

"Okay, let me get some shoes on."

The dog hops about in approval, but he becomes distracted again when his phone indicates an incoming text.

It's from her. She lets him know how the last few weeks have been nice for her, and that she hopes it continues.

Despite the fact he feels the same way, he realizes he doesn't have any idea what he is doing, and it scares him. All the uncertainty, the high level of emotionality, the heat is on inferno mode, and he doesn't know if he can possibly handle it.

thirty-eight

the days now go by faster than ever before. There was a time when they were much slower, and he wonders exactly why.

Funny, when one is a kid, they want to do the adult things and it takes forever to get there, yet once you're there, fuck if it isn't life in high gear, and the years speed by like minutes.

He trains, he works, and he looks forward to seeing her. The month has passed in hyper speed, as if it has been only an hour.

They seem to have settled into a ritual when they see each other. Wednesday and Saturday are the designated times. They go out, they have fun, they wake up next to each other (if they sleep), they text every day, they speak on the phone. Rinse and repeat.

They are obviously seeing each other, yet it all goes unsaid. Clearly, there is no reason to play the field, as no one in any field, of any kind, could measure up to the one they are already on. This field is working for both of them just fine.

Yet it is all very confusing, as with most people, both have made a career at ephemeral relationships. Yes, there are those rare couples who manage to beat the test of time, but let's face it, they are all too few and very far between.

He is confused because he simply didn't see this coming. He wonders if he is beyond foolish for not having such foresight. When he meditates on it, he realizes he should have known better. He figures that since that they had never crossed that line, he hadn't considered what would ever happen if they went over it. Now that they had, it sure was obvious.

They had always had good friend chemistry. Perhaps their encounters had been too far apart to realize that they shared a sense of humor. That he liked a woman who could make him laugh. Physically, it was insane, both full of passion and drive, although, as per usual, he wondered if that would last. It never did. He had experienced this before: women thrilled at his enthusiasm for a few months only to be annoyed by it not long after. Then again, this seemed different, but he questioned what *this* was.

He wasn't going to complain, because whatever was happening was bringing him joy.

She misses him. The thought of him made her happy, but also caused grave concern. She has kept things going with him despite her multiple misgivings. Then again, she knew her propensity to overthink and wonders if her misgivings weren't misguided.

Where is this going?

Since her divorce, her rate of success beyond a day or even a week had not been exactly high. Mostly, she found fault in her prospective suitors, well, not mostly, it was total. She can't help it if she's picky. Why shouldn't she get what she wants?

Then again, it wasn't uncommon for her to switch gears often. What she wanted was a fluid situation. Sometimes, upon getting something she wanted, came the notion that she didn't want it anymore. She wasn't the first with such interchangeable feelings, nor would she be the last.

But even she questioned why she kept second guessing it. It was, after all, as nice as could be, whatever it was. Why would anyone waste precious time wondering what would go wrong? She was constantly having to talk herself down.

Such is apparently the gist of human behavior. In the end, the species were nothing more than emotional masochists.

And now she realizes that she wants more. She doesn't want to scare him off, but needs are needs. She wonders if she has always wanted more from him. She liked the way he was in some respects, and those respects were what she both wanted and needed. Then again, what about the other things she knew about him that she wasn't sure she could deal with?

No, no, no. I want this.

She finds herself asking questions that have no definite answers, but what did?

She has always wanted a future with someone, and she has certainly considered the thought of him. But he was older than she and had the on-again-off-again rapport with someone else, all contributing to a lack of full consideration. Until now, that is.

thirty-nine

they are sitting side by side, sort of. There is a gargoyle in between them as they perch, looking down from the Cathedral of Notre Dame. He drapes his arm around the stone creature, as if posing for a selfie.

All three stare out at the Seine below like they are all made of stone. Even though they are far from anyone who could hear them speak, they still communicate on their own private mind frequency.

"This is what you wanted?" she asks.

"I'm not sure what you mean," he responds.

"Oh, please, of course you do."

"You are tired of the game?"

"I wish something would happen."

"Something is! Romance is afoot. They are libel to be famous lovers if this keeps up," he remarks.

"Interesting."

"It is? I thought you were bored."

"Oh, I am," she admits.

"As per usual, I can't follow your logic."

"The stakes are high; do you not agree?"

"Yes." There is a hint of a smile as she absently pets the gargoyle.

"You plan to shake up the board?"

"Indeed."

"What have you in mind?"

"I'm not sure just yet, but all this bliss is too much to stand. It needs a test."

"I'm just not sure why you can't let it take its natural course. All honeymoons end. It is inevitable."

"So is death, yet humans speed that along, too, in such a hurry to get to the next life."

"Not all do that," he comments, more optimistic than usual.

"Most do. *Most*."

He shrugs and resumes looking out at the river while she pets the gargoyle, plotting and scheming as she does.

forty

she is there, but also not. The woman is talking to her, and she appears to be listening, but what she is doing is looking down at her phone to see if he has texted. She is becoming an expert at the surreptitious look-see. At least, that's what she tells herself.

He had texted earlier, asking if she had tried some restaurant she had never heard of. When he found out it was new for her, he said he would like to take her, she said that sounded nice and agreed. What she didn't like was waiting days to see him. There was a smidge of resentment that she hoped wouldn't grow to whatever the opposite of smidge was.

She was thinking about him all the time—one might use the word *obsessed* if one was bold enough. It wasn't unlike her; she loved love. She always wanted it to be different, but then it never was. Each new romance brought a hope that sprung eternal. For some reason, she felt more hopeful this time, or was it more and more hopeful each time?

It didn't matter, whatever it was, this was the zenith of love mountain. Mount LovEverest.

The customer asks something, and she snaps out of it.

"I must be losing my hearing," she says apologetically.

"You just seem distracted," the customer says.

She smiles.

"You are seeing someone!"

She is caught and she knows it. They all know she has been friends with him for years, which is why she has held back saying anything, as she normally would have told everyone, because in the community she runs in, if she told one person, they all would know regardless. She may as well tell everyone, and now she will have to.

She is surprised that her client thinks he is a good choice, although she doesn't quite buy in to the notion he was indeed of her choice. It was as though fate had intervened, and they had just happened.

Sure, she had thought about it before, but now it was happening, and it seemed like it was supposed to happen. It didn't feel as if it were in her sphere of control. She hadn't realized how alarming that would be. She'd been allowing him to control how the relationship went, and she wasn't that kind of woman normally.

But there was more to it than that. He was older, had no children. She was younger and had kids, and she wondered for only a whisper of a moment if that would be an issue.

He never wanted kids.

She didn't know why it came up for her. He knew she had kids, but their friendship, and subsequent romantic involvement, had never gone there. Stakes were raised, and she realized at some point she would have to admit that she wanted more, both for herself as well as from him. Maybe it was still too early, maybe things didn't need definition.

But maybe they do.

forty-one

he started to think, and when he did, he knew that was trouble, because thinking on it, especially at the exponential rate that he was, meant that there was more and more at stake.

He was both surprised and not surprised at what was occurring. She once mentioned their age difference awhile back, although she hadn't mentioned it since they had become physical. Perhaps it was their shared enthusiasm for the act that had quelled that argument against him.

To him, age was just a number. Sure, he had years on her, but that didn't matter one iota. In his head, he was twenty-five and he stayed that age perpetually. Sometimes he felt his age; he had to limit basketball in his late thirties, but only after winning back-to-back championships in not-so-easy New York City leagues.

He didn't want to, but he knew he had to. The recovery times had become longer and harder. Banging out with men stronger and younger had taken a toll. So, he would have to find another sport eventually.

He played tennis and racquetball too, but that dinged him up, as well. He had to play through, because that's what he did, despite his assigned age number being twice what was in his head.

Still, he knew he had been down this road before. It was too soon, but fate could give a fuck if you were ready.

You have been given a gift. Take it or lose it.

He knows there is something to this, more than friends with really brilliant benefits. He had never been friends with someone before elevating it to a romantic level. Yes, sure, they saw each other a few times a week, but it was dating. They were seeing each other, and he knew that sooner than later, maybe before he was ready, he would have to up his relationship game or face losing her.

What the fuck am I doing?

Doesn't matter. There are no rules, only consequences.

He feels guilty. He was having fun again. He didn't mourn much. Then again, he had given the last relationship every chance and then some to become mutually acceptable. It hadn't worked and now something was working well, it was happy, it was great to see her, to think about her, to touch her skin, to grab her and kiss her, to caress her hand across a dinner table.

I'm in trouble. Fuck, fuck, and double fuck.

He is both lost and found. It's the redundant conundrum. The wonderful warmth of sharing life with a specific person, as opposed to the freedom of doing whatever the moment called for.

He doesn't know. He has heard timing is an essential part of relationship success, and he knows there is a modicum of truth to that, but life was a game of adjustments, and he could manage his issues of emotional proximity, but would that be enough?

She is feeling like a girlfriend without the title, but it had been a month of seeing each other and now Christmas is coming. She asks him what he was doing.

Nothing.

She doesn't ask anymore, but he senses the nihilist answer wasn't floating.

The silence was loud, pounding him relentlessly, and no amount of imbibing could wash out silence.

This may be for the best, moving forward.

He once told her, "We are the sum of our experiences." And while that may be true, he wondered if one could change the experience and adjust the outcome, at least emotionally, or did we always hold desperately onto our crutches and bask in the safety of our damages?

Of course, it wasn't that simple, the warm blanket of the devil we knew was sometimes our best friend. He didn't like holidays, especially this one.

Scrooge 2.0.

There was comfort in being alone at this time. No gratuitous gift-giving or pretending you like the people you gather with at this time because of some genealogical obligation.

Perhaps its didn't matter. She had let him be, and she should have known why after years of hearing why.

Then there was the push-pull inside him. Was she his girlfriend? Could he handle that now? Was it too deep to assign a label? They weren't just friends anymore, but everything was so nice. This was a time to enjoy not constantly stress over. Yet he does.

What have I gotten myself into?

He hadn't planned this, but now it seemed he may have painted himself into a corner, the overthinking parade was on an endless loop. Maybe it was just the season, maybe this was normal for him, but what he didn't know was that the stakes of the game were about to change, and he had no choice in the matter.

forty-two

they sit in the Luxembourg Gardens at a small table with tiny espresso cups in front of them that are not for sipping. They are accoutrements, to fit an image, which is odd as no one seems to notice them, yet they notice everyone.

In fact, that's what they are doing: sitting and observing, judging, and not drinking espresso.

They watch a couple who walk hand in hand, saying nothing, relying only on their body language. They turn toward each other so frequently one may think they were concerned they may be missing something.

"Annoying," she says.

"How so?"

"It's ephemeral."

"How can you be so sure?"

She turns to him, expressing her incredulousness at his statement. He is disquieted by the fact she made a point to look at him.

"So, you say the same about our experiment?" he asks.

"You are well aware how it ends."

"I am aware what it is, but how can forever end?"

There is a vague sense of a shrug, although no motion from her can really be detected at all. Neither of them, really. That's the secret;

they move at speeds so fast that even if they could be perceived, it would never register on any human radar.

Yet they are on each other's detection systems, that's for sure. As if they always have been and always will be.

forty-three

he has planned a date for Christmas Eve. This is their day. He got her something small, a display of acknowledgment that she has engaged in as well.

I'm here.

He reads the text that he was anticipating receiving. He has the small gift bag, filled with a scented candle and some high-end tea, and he hopes she likes it. He feels awkward, not obligated, yet still weird with the offering. What gift is enough to acknowledge her presence in his life without it being too much or too little?

Coming.

She sits in the car reading the text, catching the smile run across her face before it becomes too wide. In the back seat, she has a hand-poured candle made to give him. He has lots of candles, so she thought that it works without seeming too girlfriendish.

She superfluously reapplies her ruby red lipstick. She stops as soon as she sees the garage door begin to open and hides the makeup as if she had done something wrong.

She smiles as he comes toward her and then moves to the passenger side door. This scene has become all too familiar, her picking him up for dates, the two of them canoodling in some corner at some restaurant, making other patrons either jealous or annoyed, sometimes both.

They both wore black, she a jumper, he a shirt, jacket, and slacks. It was if they were in sync. Certainly, they matched in a fashion sense, but it was clear they matched in other ways, as well. The friendship was beyond reproach, although he thought it an asset in the past, but also, he attributed whatever heightened experience they were having currently to that base and wondered if that would guarantee future success.

She didn't agree so much. She didn't want whatever was happening to be characterized as friendship at all, ever again, even though he understood his point. So, they matched and kind of didn't on occasion. Neither was complaining.

They share a dusted kiss, as she warned him of her freshly painted lips. Not that he didn't notice. In fact, that made him feel the pang of an invitation.

She wipes his lips after, and he looks at her.

"What?" she asks.

"Not a good color on me?"

She reaches into her clutch and procures the makeup and hands it to him.

"Apply it yourself!"

"You think I won't?"

She laughs and puts the container back.

They park near the entrance of the restaurant, which he explains used to be an inn. He isn't sure if it's still a place to stay, but he has eaten here before, and it was delicious. It's a restaurant that is one of many in a chef's cadre of places, which he enjoyed in his previous life as a city boy.

He opens the door for her as they enter, and they both notice that they are being observed. Perhaps it is the attractive couple both draped in black, or perhaps it is that glow they feel on the inside, shining its way out. She looks at him for an answer that he does not have.

He shrugs and squeezes her hand, which helps them both renew focus as they are led to their table. They are seated in their usual spot, regardless of restaurant: a corner where they can watch the world, which also appears to be watching them.

He looks at the cocktail menu and orders them two drinks. When the order arrives, he lifts his glass.

"Salut."

A clink is followed by sips of deliciousness.

"How do always you know what I will like?" she asks coquettishly.

"I try and pay attention, hope for the best . . ."

"So far so good," she says, taking a healthy sip.

"Ooooh," he coos looking the menu.

"What did you see?"

"Lobster fra diavolo."

"What's that?" she asks. "You know what, never mind, I think you may know better what I like than I do."

"It's a spicy sauce used on seafood usually. I think you will like it."

She smiles and nods, the waiter comes, and he orders another round of drinks and food.

She feels close him. *Closer.*

"If you want to come up to my place tomorrow afternoon . . . it's me and the kids, if you like."

He nods uncomfortably. It isn't about her, the discomfort. It is what she is offering.

Family.

He catches himself wringing his hands at the table, so does she. She places her hands over his.

"I remember you saying you didn't enjoy holidays."

"I really don't, especially this time of year. Thanksgiving and Christmas. I guess my experience hasn't been so great."

She nods in understanding, but it still throws him. She was aware when they were friends this was the case.

She just wants to include you. It's nice, be grateful.

He takes another swig of his drink, relieved that the food has come and the moment has passed. He thanks the waiter, who has no idea that the thanks are for multiple reasons.

The food, drinks, and ambience are all good, but the company is unparalleled. They laugh and smile.

"Let's take a picture," he suggests.

"Hang on," she says, making sure she is properly coifed.

He waits patiently, and finally, when she is ready, she nestles up to him. He raises his phone in the air and captures the moment. This is their first photo together, and as soon as he lowers the phone, she asks to see it.

"We look good together, May I air drop it to myself?"

"Of course."

She hands him back his phone and picks up hers, resuming her smile and staring at the good-looking couple in the photo.

He smiles at the notion of her happiness.

"How did we not know this before?" he asks.

"I had an idea," she said, putting down the phone and looking at him.

"You did?"

"You didn't?"

"I wasn't debating the attraction, but if I had thought we'd be like this, I would have dropped everything," he admits.

"Certainly different than you were used to."

He doesn't respond. He knows she is well versed in his past and the proximity to his last relationship. He is also aware of her sensitivity to it.

"This is about us," he says finally.

"Sorry, I tend to overthink on occasion."

"Don't, I get where it comes from, but this has been and is really nice for me. I just didn't see it coming."

"Let's go home," she suggests.

He asks for and pays the bill in record speed.

forty-four

She lies in bed next to him as he sleeps. She isn't sure if it is Saigon, or him, but someone is snoring lightly. The dog has fallen asleep on his master's chest, therefore making it difficult to discern.

She realizes she's slightly jealous of the dog. She wants to be nestled on him. Then she wonders if the dog slept on him when she wasn't there.

She knew she had to leave and change costumes from girlfriend to mom. Was she a girlfriend? He had said something in the heat of passion, after several drinks, after smoking a joint.

Does that count?

She didn't know why she questioned what was going on so much, but she did know she wanted some clarity.

It's been a month.

She looked at the dog, comfortable and zonked out, but the snoring was coming from her maybe boyfriend.

She wants to wake him up. It's the only part of Christmas they will be spending together, and she is on the clock. She watches him sleep for a while, hoping he will wake up, but he doesn't, and she loses hope and rests her head back on the pillow. She looks at the clock on her phone.

Half an hour.

She doesn't want to leave. She wishes he had taken her up on her offer to spend Christmas with her and her family.

Too soon?

He obviously never started his own family. He didn't ask much about kids, and he has a dog.

She was overthinking again, and she knew it. It had only been a month and change. They weren't even labeling themselves a couple just yet, although he had started to hint at the concept. She knew she wanted to have some semblance of a family. That was important to her.

The dog wakes up and she watches as he awakens his master surreptitiously, first nudging him with his nose, then licking his face and finally, when that has limited success, he jumps off the bed and barks at him.

"Ssshhhh," she attempts.

Then the dog barks at her. He wakes up.

"Quiet," she tries.

"It's okay, he just wants breakfast," he says.

She watches as he lumbers out of bed to feed the dog. She catches herself let out a long sigh.

Should I shower?

Should I lie here naked and hope he comes back?

She does throw the sheets off, exposing herself. She touches her skin, proud of how soft she feels. Before she knows it, she is touching herself all over.

"Starting without me?" he says, coming in the room.

She keeps touching herself, a bit turned on that she has been caught, a bit turned on that he seems to like catching her, and really turned on that he is joining her.

He touches himself while he watches her as long as he can take it before he needs to be inside her. They can't help it. The magnetism draws them close.

They are startled by the alarm on her phone that goes off.

Shit.

"Shit," he says aloud.

The hot frenzy comes to an abrupt halt, much to the disappointment of both participants.

"Fuck, I forgot to let the dog in," he says, rushing off.

She sighs. She has been left alone a second time, and her alarm has pulled a partial cock block—and the dog is also a cock blocker! She gets up and starts the shower, and by the time she gets out, both Saigon and her man are back.

"Why don't you come spend some time with us today?" she asks.

He just nods, and she knows her plea will most likely go unanswered.

"I'm late," she says, kissing him.

"I know," he says, breaking the embrace. "I'll walk you out."

forty-five

he misses her, but at the same time, he feels a modicum of relief. He was glad to have spent the night with her, but mostly he wanted to have a makeshift workout and then numb his distaste of the holiday.

He has some coffee and a protein bar and then goes into his basement for some pullups and pushups. He wonders if he is being an asshole for multiple reasons: one, for training on a major holiday when gyms aren't even open, and two, for not going to her house even for a little while.

He works up a decent sweat, trying to physically work through the mental angst. It has a limited effect that he knows he can further suppress with weed, tequila, and a Xanax he has been saving for a special occasion. This was that occasion.

He finishes and makes his way upstairs to let Saigon out again. He steps out on the deck as the dog tries to catch a squirrel that hadn't seen him coming. As fast as the dog is, his prey is faster and spryer.

Saigon chased him right up to the tree, even made a leap at the squirrel's tail and barked at him, as if to say "One of these days I will get you."

He watches his canine buddy make the failed hunting attempt. He is surprised that, for Christmas in New England, it was temperate.

He takes a deep breath as if believing that, when he exhales, the weight of his world would all be lifted. When that fails, he grabs the half a joint that he had noticed sitting all alone in the ashtray on the grill stand. He ignites the grill to light the joint and smokes it to the nub.

He stands on the deck, staring out at nothing. Saigon races up the stairs, and he regains focus. The dog stares at his master and he looks back at him.

"Cookie?"

Saigon jumps on him in a show of encouragement.

"Yeah, I agree."

They go inside and he gives the dog a treat then rummages around in the fridge for something himself. He thinks about bacon and eggs, but he is saving that. It's the one tradition he is down with.

As much as he dislikes the holiday—the faux caring and gift-giving was what he saw as a ridiculous and obligatory tradition—the food after, however. . . . The fluffy eggs, crisp bacon, fat bagels slathered in whipped cream cheese and preserves.

He snaps out of the food fantasy and grabs another protein bar, saving the last bastion of holiday-ness for later. He showers and finds his pill container that reads, "Don't mix with alcohol.'"

"You don't mean that!" he says to the bottle.

He takes the pill and then makes himself a drink.

I'm sure it's just a suggestion.

Amid making the libation, he takes a long pull off the bottle. It is tequila, but smooth, and between the weed, the pill, and the booze, he's feeling warm and slightly fuzzy. He smokes some more and puts on the football game, which he is thrilled is on Christmas day. He looks at his phone and sees that she had texted.

I'm here if you change your mind.

It was sweet and inviting, not what he was used to. He is warm from the mixture of booze, weed, and one happy pill. He lounges on his couch, grateful that a football game is coming on and that he can be lazy and alone.

He does think of her and realizes that she contributed to the warmth he was feeling, too. He is grateful for her in his life, he always had been, but he also isn't sure what he is doing or who it would land. She seems to be okay with it, hasn't said anything, hasn't made demands. It's been nice, relaxing. Or is that the Xanax talking?

He zones out to the game on his couch until the hunger and thirst pangs became too much to bear. He begins cooking his Christmas breakfast.

She texts him again, asking what he is doing. He gives her the quick version via text, and then she asks what he is doing the next day.

Probably just going to train in the morning . . .

She looks at his text, a bit disappointed. Her children run about with the delights a child feels with the procurement of a new toy. She wants to share that—it is a missing piece in her puzzle—and she wonders if he is it.

His stance on holidays was the first thing she could see as a major difference between them. She wonders if she has been blinded by the whirlwind romance, if that's even what this was. He feels like a boyfriend, it almost feels like it was preordained, or maybe it had always been waiting to be.

How could there be such dichotomy? Perhaps the cracks in the dam were beginning to show? Or perhaps she was doing what she does when she has too much time to think.

She understands it is early and undefined. She is going to be reasonable. Let him be, for now.

She surreptitiously makes a margarita while her kids run about playing with both opened and unopened gifts. Before she realizes it, the drink is gone. She looks at her phone, seeing if he has had a change of heart, and when it doesn't appear that he has, she makes another drink.

Why not? Where do I have to go?

She feels a pang of guilt for leaving him alone, but she recognizes that he seems to want it that like this. It isn't her way—she likes the idea of family, and holidays, and Christmas cheer.

Absently, she finds that she has polished off her second margarita. She isn't present, and that makes her feel guilty, as well.

Guilt, guilt, and more guilt, and only the power of tequila to numb it.

She decides to limit her intake, hope that the kids tire themselves out and she can forget that she is alone, but not exactly alone, or that something will clear up and she will feel on solid ground in some aspect of life.

She wakes up later in her bed, forgetting how she got there, one of her kids on either side. She chugs some water that has been sitting on her nightstand for lord knows how long, tasting the time's worth of dust that seems to have mixed itself in.

She looks her phone to see texts, but none from him, which is what she was hoping for. She sighs, plops back down in between child bookends, and lays awake, lost in too many thoughts.

forty-six

he wakes up groggy with Saigon nudging him. He groans as he rises, lumbering in the kitchen to make coffee and let the dog out. He makes Saigon his breakfast, and by the time he lets him inside, the dog is ready to consume it. Dogs may have little sense of time, except when it is time to eat. Then, they are timekeepers at the gates of dawn.

It's just past seven, but his little cocktail had him out early. He remembers falling asleep on the sofa watching the game, but he woke up in bed, the living room television off. It is unclear how that came to be.

Saigon finishes his meal as if it had never been there, the bowl looks so clean, it echoes that notion. Unlike his dog, he isn't so hungry, not a morning eater, but he needs fuel beyond the coffee.

An hour or so later, he decides to get to the gym and begrudgingly grabs a protein bar but does not eat it. He leaves the dog with fresh water and grabs his bag, filling it with a water of his own.

The coffee has not kicked in the way he had hoped. Everything seems slower. He throws his car into gear and leaves the house.

The roads seem more sinuous than normal. Such are country roads to be sure, but he should be on autopilot in terms of navigation. He's still groggy, and he is a bit sloppy on the road, but it's early so there are no consequences.

He comes to the end of one backwoods road. He is surprised to see heavy two-way traffic. He looks at the dash clock. It reads 8:59.

The day after Christmas? People must be in a rush to escape their families.

It seems like forever, him sitting at the shitty intersection. People come flying around curves from both directions, and he must negotiate all such assholes to be pointed in the correct direction to meet his destination.

The thing is he will never get there.

When he finally pulls out, the landscaping truck that came screaming around the corner smashes into him, sending the car into the woods.

When he comes to, he hears a voice on an emergency system in his shitty car that apparently has detected the accident. He doesn't remember getting hit.

"Are you injured?" the nebulous female voice asks.

He doesn't know. He feels no pain, but that is ephemeral. He sees he is covered in glass from the driver's side window, and that it is smashed in. He can't open the door.

"I can't move," he ekes out in response.

"Help is on the way," she assures him.

He isn't assured. Although he feels no pain, he knows he is injured, as he cannot move, not entirely.

He hears the sirens.

Police? Ambulance?

"Are you still with me?" the voice asks.

"Yes."

"You may have lost consciousness for a bit, but the medics are on the way. Is anyone else in the vehicle?"

"No, I am alone."

The ambulance comes, and they adroitly see that they must go in from the passenger side. They open the passenger's door and a medic leans in.

"Can you move?"

He shakes his head. "No."

"We have to get him from the back!" the medic yells to his support team.

He looks back and watches as they open the back passenger's side door. It is nerve racking, and he isn't scared, but he probably should be. Adrenaline is keeping the damage done deceptive.

The medics slide in a small board to help lift him out on. They lower the passenger's front seat to slide the plastic board in.

"We are going to get you out of there now," the lead medic announces.

The plastic board is angled in awkwardly.

"Still not much on movement?"

"I don't think so."

"I mean, if you can help us slide you on it, may be easier for you."

"Easier?"

"We don't know the extent of your injuries, so . . ."

"That makes two of us," he quips.

Then the pain comes, shooting through his soul as if a demon who lived within was tearing his way out.

"Stop!" he screamed.

"I know it hurts, but we gotta get you out of there," the medic said, ignoring him.

He must have passed out from the pain, because the next thing he knows, he's in motion. The ambulance is moving.

"Hey, there you are!" the EMT says.

He manages a groan. The pain is dull and throbbing. He wants to sit up and look at his left leg, but when he does, he screams.

"That would be broken ribs, if I could guess, but just try and relax. We will get you settled and find out what is going on once we land."

Broken ribs. Saigon.

"Do you have my phone?" he asks.

"If it was in the car, they will have it."

"I have to get someone to take care of my dog."

"I understand. I have dogs, too. We just gotta make sure you are stable, then we can find your phone."

He nods. The pain is dull and pulsating. He knows he is hurt, but he can't tell how badly. The EMT seems concerned, but also isn't saying much. He starts to sweat. Panic is setting in.

They get to the hospital and get him out of the ambulance and into the ER. They cut him out of his sweatshirt. He starts to complain, but they tell him they must diagnose his wounds. They take X-rays and then move him into the hallway, where he is immobile on a gurney.

A male nurse comes by and tells him he has five broken ribs and a broken pelvis. He asks about the pain, which now feels worse after being told he is broken.

"I will get you something to help."

A police officer comes up to him as the nurse leaves. He hands him a plastic bag with his phone and wallet in it.

"I'm issuing you a ticket, for pulling out in front of a car."

"Are you kidding? That truck was going ninety miles an hour."

The cop hands him the ticket. "You can fight it," he says walking away.

He can't believe the flippant attitude. *The guys speeding in the landscaping truck got away scot-free.*

The nurse comes back and gives him two pills and a small cup of water.

"What's this?"

"Pain pills, good ones, called oxycontin."

"I hate pills."

"You don't want them? You have substantial injuries that warrant these."

He looks at the pills. Two little fuckers that promise to take away the pain. He takes them and then the water and gulps them down.

"You can get some every few hours. They are going to admit you for more evaluation," he tells him.

"How long?"

"No idea. Depends on what they want to do to you. A resident will be by to explain more."

"Thanks."

He takes his phone out of the plastic. There are a few texts from her, and he debates what to say. She will notice if he is silent for too long.

While he debates, he texts his trusted Saigon caregiver. He explains what has happened and asks if she can help him until he can figure out what is happening.

She calls him and ensure him that she can, asks if he is okay. He doesn't know, perhaps that is the meds kicking in. He feels awkward and tells her there is a doctor coming to talk to him—a lie designed to get off the phone.

He doesn't know why, but he is dreading the text to her. He figures he needs to say something, so he texts her and tells her about the accident.

What???!!! Are you okay?

Before he can text back, a call comes in. He gives her more details.

"I will be there as soon as I can," she tells him.

"No, it's okay. I know you are with your family. I will be fine."

"You are pissing me off right now."

"I am?"

"Yes, I said I will be there as soon as I can."

This time, he has the brains not to argue.

forty-seven

he lies in bed pathetically, because when you have crushed ribs and a shattered pelvis, there is little room to be anything but pathetic. People come and go to check his temperature and blood pressure what seems like every minute. These are the machinations on the road leading to insanity.

They have told him he will need to heal and learn to walk again. They also said that ribs have to heal on their own, as does the pelvis, so likely they will watch him for a few days, and he will be sent home or to an outpatient rehab.

She comes in as the persistent vital sign tester is done with what seems to be an hourly annoyance.

When she hugs him, he yelps in pain.

"Broken ribs, five of them."

"I'm sorry, I didn't mean—"

"I forget myself, and then I sneeze."

She asks what happened and he tells her. She is sweet and tender. It is exactly what he hadn't realized he needed. She sits carefully on the hospital bed, being perfect in that moment. They both realize this but say nothing. Words can't do any more than what is being done just fine on its own.

They are interrupted. A team of people enter: a man, mid-thirties, a cadre of younger men and women standing behind him.

"So, we are a bit concerned about some of the damage done to your pelvis. We have contacted a trauma specialist to see if we need to take the surgical option."

"What now?" he asked, suddenly alarmed.

He is not good at having things done to him, doesn't like strangers poking and prodding, certainly not rummaging around his insides. He looks at her nervously. He thinks he is hiding his fear, but he is terrible at hiding any emotion. She senses his anxiety and sits next to him carefully, as to avoid accidentally aggravating his injuries. She squeezes his wrist, hoping she is hitting an acupressure point that will calm. She discovered this with her own nervousness. It seems to work.

"We are going to try and get you up and moving, too. Physical therapy will be in to see you soon. Any questions?"

He probably should have lots of them, but his nerves have him drawing a blank. Finally, he shakes his head, and the cadre of interns dissipate.

She watches his concerned face, which has an occasional stress twitch. She doesn't know what to say or do to help him manage the anxiety he is clearly experiencing.

"They said with these injuries they just let them heal, so it's a little nerve-wracking, the idea of surgery."

"Hear what they have to say first. I think it's good they are making sure the treatment is the right course."

He looks at her gratefully. Of course, she is right.

"I appreciate you coming, but I know you have other obligations. I didn't mean for you to run to me. I just didn't want you to worry if you didn't hear anything."

"Don't be ridiculous," she says. "I can't stay long anyway, but I want to know what is going on. You have someone who can look after Saigon?"

He explains the dog walker.

"I can stay the nights I am free."

He smiles at the gesture. "Like you said, let's see what they say, how long I have to be here, but that is really nice of you to offer."

He is both glad she is there and uncomfortable with how reliable she is. It is new for him, and he isn't sure he is ready for that, but he can't say so.

"I have to get back, but I will come tomorrow."

"I am okay. I know you have work."

"Sometimes you need to know when to stop talking," she deadpans.

She kisses him. "It will be okay. I will make sure of that," she tells him as she leaves.

He waits as long as he can hold it, but eventually his eyes start leaking.

forty-eight

he calls her later to tell her the news. His pelvis has crumbled, and the trauma surgeon has advised a surgical fix. He has to do it or he may never walk right again.

She asks him what he will do, and she is surprised to hear he will go with the surgical option. She is more surprised to hear him admit that he is scared, but he is in a lot of pain, and this hopefully will get him back to normal. They have told him it will be hard, but the physical challenge isn't what worries him. The surgery does, but once it's done, it's done.

She tells him she will come for a few hours the next day. He holds back saying it isn't necessary; he has learned that lesson. Instead, they say their goodbyes, and he zones out to the Food Network.

He will be zoned out like this for a while. The physical therapists want to get him up and moving, and that will be on tap soon enough before surgery.

His broken ribs ache, and pain shoots through his left side if he forgets his current state or sneezes. His tolerance for pain is low, a self-admitted baby. She is much stronger than him in that regard, and he is slightly embarrassed, yet this is who he is.

She is worried about him. Her instinct to protect him and care for him has kicked in more than she bargained for. It is causing her more stress than she wanted or needed. When the next day comes, she hears his screams from the hallway. When she gets to his room, she sees they are trying to get him to stand. It isn't going well.

He sees her come in and asks if they can take a break.

"You need to move," one of the physical therapists says.

He sits on the bed with obvious exhaustion. "Hi," he manages weakly.

"Hi," she says, gently sitting next to him.

She kisses him on the cheek and the slight weight of her pressing on him makes him groan in pain.

"That bad?"

"Let's try and get you up in the chair. It's not good for you not to sit up for so long."

She stresses out as he screams and yelps in tremendous pain. It as if she can feel it herself, like somehow, they are one, but she tries not to show it. It takes what seems an eternity to get him slid from bed to chair. He looks incredibly frail; the pain still lives on his face even though the screaming has stopped.

"I don't want you to see me like this," he admits, shifting uncomfortably in his chair.

"So, what, I am not supposed to see you at all?"

"I'm not used to it; I have been on my own for a while."

"Well, you aren't alone now."

He doesn't enjoy what feels like helplessness, but her devotion and persistence warms his soul, and the angst briefly retreats. Then he sneezes, and he is back to being uncomfortably vulnerable.

"Can you ask for the therapist? I think I need to get back into bed," he asks her.

"Sure," she says, rushing up.

He screams in his mind, knowing full well those internal howls will soon bubble to the surface.

forty-nine

they are back in the gardens at Versailles, this time by the pond. They watch the images in the pool of people in a hospital in some place far from where they are. It as if they are watching a movie, but the images are being projected on water rather than a screen.

There are people around them, walking about the gardens and completely unaware there is a movie of sorts playing that they cannot see, nor can they see the beings watching it. No one can see the invisible, or if they can, they do not betray the gift.

The two beings sit together, watching the movie intently until she looks away in disgust.

"What?" he inquires.

"What are we doing?"

"Playing the game, you suggested it."

"I mean, what's the point?"

"To amuse ourselves, obviously!"

"This is boring. We should have killed him."

"That would defeat the purpose."

"I suppose."

"You are impossible," he suggests.

She shrugs.

"Perhaps we could make it more interesting," he suggests.

She looks at him with obvious interest. "What do have you in mind?"

"Let's be capricious."

"Let's," she says with a smile.

fifty

there are still days before the surgery. He wishes there weren't. The pain has set in, and despite the fact he is scared shitless, he is desperate for relief.

She has been relentless in her care for him, despite having to manage her own needs. It is clear to him she is planting her flag, and he is both grateful and fearful.

Like clockwork, she comes at designated visiting hours and stays the full two hours. She is insistent on speaking with his care team, to make sure there is something he is not telling her. He looks frail. It amazes her how trauma and lack of movement can devastate a person so rapidly.

She leaves reluctantly. He's in bad shape, worse than either of them realizes. Her worry is a bit consuming, and therefore, off-putting. Yet she feels intensely strong about the situation; she will do everything she possibly can to help.

They try to get him moving again. They are concerned about the consequences of not moving. The pain is excruciating, and the entire floor hears his suffering. He begs them to stop torturing him. When they agree, they warn him of more problems, fluid building in his lungs and drowning him from the inside out.

It scares him, but the pain is overwhelming. They are giving him morphine, but it feels as if he is becoming tolerant. This is all he needs. He is counting the time between bouts of relief. Even though he is giant baby, his desperation trumps all.

She is in and out for the days leading up to the big day. She is beyond supportive; despite his constant frustration, she refuses to budge from her protective perch. She sees he is in pain; she sees that he is scared.

She leaves the afternoon before the next morning's surgery. She says she will be there when he wakes up. He nods nervously. He waits until she leaves and then inexplicably bursts into tears. His anxiety has him wondering if he will die.

He gathers himself and eats some of the Thai food she brought him. His appetite is close to nothing, which is odd. The lack of walks in the woods or gym has him not needing the normal fuel.

Someone comes in for the billionth time to take vitals. He hates the regular intrusion. He refuses and is bitchy about it. This is followed by the coup de grâce when a male nurse comes in.

"I'm here to put your catheter in," he says

"What?"

"You are getting a catheter."

"No, I most definitely am not."

"I know what I'm doing," he says, trying to inspire confidence.

"I am not debating that; I just don't want a tube shoved in my penis."

"No one does. Trust me, you'd rather have me do it."

He sighs and then agrees after being scared off the alternative. It is beyond painful. Death seems a better option. When the pain subsides, he takes the last sip of water he is allowed. He hopes the pangs of thirst and hunger he feels is worse than the surgery will be.

The night is sleepless, and he is scared.

He is awake when they wheel him to pre-op. He looks forward to not being broken physically. He looks forward to having a milkshake. In his insomnia, he decided the best reward for being a big boy is a chocolate shake.

They wheel his bed into the pre-op room, where he is met by the surgeon. He is given paperwork to sign that absolves them if they fuck up.

Comforting.

"We will see you in there," the surgeon says gleefully, absolution in hand.

He is getting more and more nervous; something tells him it won't go well.

The anesthesiologist thankfully comes to his rescue, giving him something to relax before knocking him out.

he was legally dead for three minutes. That was what the surgeon tells her. They pulled him out and revived him. He is stable, but they didn't fix him. They will have to go back in the next day.

This is no way to ring in the new year.

She's not sure why she thanks him. She has been on the brink of a full-blown panic attack for hours. They said it wouldn't take this long, then again, they probably didn't count on him dying on them either.

She is with some friends, but she isn't present. She hadn't considered the possibility that things could become so dire. The thought of losing him sent a shiver through her soul. She excuses herself and goes to the bathroom, where she turns on the water so her friends can't hear her cry.

Her face betrays her when she returns. When her friends ask, she spills her pain all over the floor, as if the dam that held back tears simply couldn't hold.

They tell her it will be okay, but she knows it's just lip service.

It should be okay now, but it isn't.

She has taken over dog care duties, and she wants to go home to Saigon and be close to the creature, as it will serve as a substitute for *him.*

The impetus surprises her because she isn't a dog person.

The creature is sweet, but he seems confused at disappearance of his master. He has also seemingly gained weight. She wonders if she and other caregivers are overfeeding and under-exercising him. She knows that he takes long walks in the woods with him.

She realizes as she thinks of him and Saigon that she doesn't know where his leash is, or if he walks him in the dead of winter.

Dead.

Three minutes.

Fuck.

He is too young to die.

No, no, no . . .

She tells her friends she needs to leave. It is early, and not the way to celebrate the new year, but it also seems not the time to celebrate anything. They will try the surgery again, hopefully death free, yet now that concept seems beyond possible.

His house feels empty without him. Saigon is happy to see her, even though he feels the weight of what has happened. Yet the dog is sweet and the only way she has to connect with him.

She feeds the dog and makes herself a margarita. She drinks about half absently, remembering how he always looks at her when she gulps her booze but says nothing. He accepts her, warts and all.

Don't die on me.

Death was not something that had touched her yet. She was lucky in that regard. Yet she knows luck runs out, death is undefeated. She looks at the dog, who has taken her spot on the bed. She has taken his spot as a result. She wonders who will care for the dog long term, then she gets mad at herself for having this thought.

Positive. He is strong.

She doesn't want the dog on the bed with her, but she is happy for the comfort of the being next to her at same time. She has asked him to keep the dog off the bed when they're in it, but he has ignored her pleas. The dog tends to nestle in between them, and she doesn't like that. But now the dog serves as ballast to him, or what is left of him.

She falls asleep, and when she wakes, she looks expectantly at her phone for a text from *him.*

There is nothing. But sometimes nothing is good.

No news is good news.

fifty-two

she fell asleep fully dressed, bed still made. Her exhaustion and booze apparently kicked in. She was groggy yet felt rested. She looked at her phone, nothing from hospital.

No news is good news.

They said that he would go back in early morning, and it was already eight o'clock.

No news . . .

The dog lays next to her as if waiting for a cue. She gets up and lets him out the door. She looks at her phone. She knows she will be staring at it all day. This is how yesterday went, but hopefully today will have a better result.

She spends the day with the dog, who seems grateful. His ballast is gone, and she realizes hers may be, too. She understands why he likes the creature. He is growing on her, despite the preconceived concept.

She is beginning to make herself crazy staring at her phone. The anticipation and the worry have built substantial momentum in the pathways of her mind. She thinks to make herself a drink but doesn't capitulate to her own weakness.

What if he needs me?

Instead, she finds the dog's leash and takes him into the winter weather. She is grateful for the movement, and the dog seems to enjoy it, as well. His house is in the woods on a quiet lane. She sees no one as she walks, and for that she is thankful. She can't help but check her phone. As it turns out, fate doesn't want her looking. She has no service on the walk.

The Universe is giving her a respite; problem is, she can't allow it to happen. When she walks about a half mile without service, she turns around and goes back to the warm safety of the Wi-Fi enabled home so that she can drive herself crazier.

Hours pass. She thinks of calling the hospital, but talks herself off that ledge. Too much time to think.

She thinks about cooking but thinks better of it. She doesn't enjoy it the way he does, and on New Year's Day, she wonders what stores are open. Instead, she orders comfort food, Thai, something that they have had together. When the food comes, she finds she cannot eat. In fact, all she can do is cry.

This is somewhat unexpected. It was not a surprise that she came with sensitivities, but she'd been unaware of how much the connection meant. Perhaps we don't tell ourselves these things until we question what would happen if that person were gone.

It is 6:00 p.m., and she still has heard nothing.

They must have started later than they wanted to . . .

Didn't they say in the morning?

She finds herself suddenly stuffing her face with chili garlic noodles when the phone does ring.

The surgeon tells her it will be a long recovery. His lung collapsed, and he is on a ventilator. The next few days will be critical.

She asks when she can see him.

"We can try for tomorrow, but he may not be conscious."

fifty-three

she is devastated to see him in the state he is in. He looks like a shadow of who he used to be, as if he could break in a billion little pieces if he were mishandled any further.

He sits in a clean room, attached to a ventilator that appears to be sucking life out of him rather than being a lifeline. He isn't conscious. It is explained to her that he needs to come to and breathe on his own for them to take him off the machine.

She insists on being let in, and they say no, multiple times, before it comes clear that they will not stop her from being next to him. When they finally give in, they make her wear a mask and scrubs.

No hazmat suits?

She gets in the room, wondering why she was in such a rush. He looks as if a small wind could blow him away.

Are all bouts with death so brutal?

He is gaunt and ashen, not such a good look. She takes a deep breath and sits next to him and holds his hand. She tells him how her day was and that she misses him. She pauses to allow him a grunt or anything that provides a sign of life, but when none comes, she tells a story about Saigon, how he chased a squirrel and almost caught the creature and seemed disappointed he didn't get rodent sashimi.

Nothing.

It as if she is looking at an empty shell, and perhaps in many ways he is. She catches herself singing in Russian. She hasn't sung in years; it is a lullaby that her sister sang to her as a child, and the last time she performed it was when her own babies were born.

He doesn't move. The machine moves his chest for him. She feels like she died a bit herself when the visit is interrupted by nursing staff. They seem annoyed that she has questions about what to expect moving forward.

"How bad is this? Will he recover? How does he get nutrition? He looks thirty pounds thinner than a week ago."

"We don't know. He is strong enough to get this far, then there is more hope than not, but we would feel better if he could breathe on his own. They give him some liquid nutrition, but as soon as he wakes up, we will get him on whatever he can tolerate."

"I will be back tomorrow," she tells them.

"We made an exception today, that's not possible."

"I will be back tomorrow."

<h1 style="text-align:center">*fifty-four*</h1>

she goes back day after day, and the day after that. Nothing changes, other than they give in when they see her coming. She is no one to be trifled with. They have learned that lesson expeditiously.

He isn't waking up. He isn't off the ventilator. He isn't doing anything but wasting away exponentially. She is helpless, and it is murder on her soul. She has spoken to everyone and everyone's direct supervisor. Nothing changes, she, and all who manage the hospital, can't control this.

She sits with him and holds his hand. She tells him what has happened to him, even though he won't remember.

He moans. It is weak, but she gets excited at this minuscule sign of life.

"Hi," she says.

Hi? For fuck's sake, guy is mostly dead for days and you offer "hi" for his Welcome Back to Consciousness party?

He moans again and holds her breast.

"You aren't as fucked up as you let on, are you?"

He starts to gasp, likely due to his breathing assistance, but that doesn't unlock his vice grip on her, as if it will be the last thing he will ever feel.

"You have to let go or you won't live to feel them again!"

She pries his hand away and runs to get a nurse. She comes back and he is done gagging. She squints to get a closer look.

"Is he?"

"Alive? Yes, he is."

"The choking, or gagging, it seemed . . . bad."

"He can't choke it out, don't worry. But he may have come to for a moment and wasn't relaxed."

"Would you be relaxed with a tube down your throat?"

"I've been choked by worse," the nurse smiles.

She isn't amused but feigns a grin.

"He will be, okay?"

"We would love it if he would stay conscious, but he's been through a lot. I don't envy the recovery."

"That means he will recover?"

The nurse crosses her fingers and leaves.

Great . . .

She sits next to him and holds his hand. She laughs as his maybe not so unconscious hand lands on her bosom again.

fifty-five

they perch on the top level of the Musée d'Orsay, watching, observing, and conspiring.

"I'm more bored than ever," she admits.

"Why? Our project is still not to your liking?"

"Not particularly interesting these days now, is it?"

"You asked for something to happen, a test. Now this displeases you?"

She just throws a look, almost human, so that if anyone in the museum could see them, they would know exactly what she meant.

Yet they are there, but not there. Surrounded by people, yet are all alone, in that regard, and solely that, they are like humans. Whatever has been left of their humanity, it is mostly gone from eons of time. People rarely change in a lifetime. The same holds true of most beings, ethereal or otherwise.

Their lives are players of a human chess game. They scoff at the idea of monotheism, even though they themselves have evolved from a human shell. It is possible, at one point, before they leveled up, they too may have believed in one almighty deity.

Now, they found humans and their beliefs beyond silly, and therefore justified using them to simply see what happened when they did whatever horrible things they could conjure. Perhaps that was the last bastion of their humanity, a penchant for destruction.

"It isn't sporting to kill him. She will just find a replacement," she says nonchalantly.

"So, the conclusion is that everyone is replaceable?"

"Maybe not to everyone, but to *her,* everyone is replaceable, but you know that already."

"That's comforting," he thinks sardonically.

"You know better. I am not here to comfort you."

"A disruptor to the core, I see," he says quasi-insulted.

"Yes, I am the total package, still old information."

He sighs almost audibly enough that a human passerby even senses it and looks at the empty space where they are, but, of course, the person cannot see.

"It's time," she says.

"Fantastic," he responds.

fifty-six

she is with him when he wakes up. He gasps, as he has been wont to do with a tube snaked down his throat for five days.

"It's okay, you can't choke," she says, taking his hand.

He looks at her, in obvious distress. She can't imagine walking up like this. She finds herself stroking his hand and hitting pressure points on his wrist and arm. It works. His choking stops and breathing normalizes.

"Do you remember anything?" she asks.

He looks at her blankly then shakes his head.

"They said you would forget, so I keep telling you."

So, she tells him again. He seems exhausted by the story and nods off. In and out of consciousness is better than no consciousness at all.

She waits for him to wake again, but he doesn't before the nurses tell her that the visit is over. They tell her that they will move him out of the clean room and into ICU. And the idea is to get him off the ventilator and start his recovery soon after.

She thanks them and leaves the hospital. She is worn down and realizes she has no food at home. She has been so preoccupied with everything else, she has neglected to feed herself or even have food in her house.

She finds herself at the store as a result. She absently leaves the car and walks into the store. She doesn't notice the man in the baseball hat and the single gold tooth, even as he smiles at her.

The man follows her into the store and watches as she looks at the various vegetable offerings in the organic section. She stops at the cucumbers and picks up some to examine them.

"Hi there," gold tooth offers.

It registers with her barely.

"I like to work out. Maybe you would like to join me?"

"What?" she says.

"I am asking you if you would be interested in working out with me. I have a membership around the corner, I can get you in," he says, smiling and showing off his single bejeweled tooth among the white ones.

She squints as if her eyes betray her.

A gold tooth?

"What do you say?" he persists.

"I say that I have my own membership," she says, walking off sans vegetables.

He follows her to the car, where she turns and gives him a look of death. He understands the nonverbal message and walks in the other direction, allowing her to escape unscathed.

She sits in her car with a range of emotions that she rather not be having. It's too much. She wonders why she started a romantic relationship with her friend.

Look where this has gotten you!

She is startled by a knocking on her car window. It is a police officer. She starts the car and rolls down the window.

"You okay?" the cop asks.

"Yeah, I must have fallen asleep."

"Have you used any drugs or alcohol?"

She looks at him as if he'd asked her if she has a penis.

"Miss, I have to ask, and I need an answer."

"No, I am apparently more tired than I believed. I am exhausted."

The cop looks at her and nods. "Okay, can you get yourself home?"

She nods and starts the car.

"Drive safe," he says as he walks off.

She drives away, and her stomach growls. She tries to remember when she last ate. It is an exercise in futility. She can't fathom when life had a hint of normalcy to it. Perhaps a goal of normal was unobtainable for everyone.

Everything seems to be failing. She has been beaten up by the recent events. She wasn't surprised by her sensitivity but is certainly frustrated by it. Where was the world of unicorns and rainbows?

Not here, there are no rainbows here.

She manages to get herself home and makes herself a celebratory drink. Her nervous system is shot, and while she knows the booze is probably a factor, but she doesn't have another way to decompress.

She sits on her deck and lights a cigarette from the pack that seems lonely on the small table where she left it.

It will get better. It has to, doesn't it?

The drinks and cigarettes serve as a ballast, and on an empty stomach, she has a buzz faster than usual. It is calming, or at the least distracting.

When she wakes up in the morning, she sees she has made a late-night snack, although given there is food all over her shirt, counter, and floor, she wonders if she actually consumed any of it. There is undercooked pasta and a jar of tomato sauce with most of what was inside on the outside of the jar, on the countertop, and on the floor.

Her head has a dull ache, and she feels slightly vertiginous. She groans as she has the double insult of being out of K-cups and having to clean up her culinary disaster substantially hungover and violently under caffeinated.

She calls the hospital, and they cannot find him. He isn't where he was, and she says that they said they had wanted to move him to ICU, and she just needed to know when *those* visiting hours were.

No hours for visiting the ICU she is told. Her head pulses harder as she explains that isn't possible given they just let her into a clean room. She is told that doesn't sound right.

Neither does losing my boyfriend.

She gives his name *again*, reminds them that he is on a ventilator, what floor she visited him, the surgeon's information. The coup de grâce is that the call is disconnected before any answer is given.

Inside, she is screaming with frustration. She looks at herself in the bathroom mirror. She feels as if she is looking at an older version of herself.

<h1 style="text-align:center">fifty-seven</h1>

when she arrives at the hospital, they have located him, but she has missed the visiting hours. She puts on her game face and opens her inner complaint department to three administrators, which turns out to be the key to an hour with him.

He is conscious but still on a ventilator. Disturbing as that is, it's still a massive improvement. He looks frail, even though he is being filled with fluids and some kind of sustenance.

He reaches out to her intermittently, gasping, as he can't seem to adjust to the tube down his throat. He stops when they achieve physical touch. He squeezes her hand to get her attention then makes the motion of writing on air.

"You want to write?"

He nods.

She moves to her backpack and fishes out a notepad and a pen. She hands him the pen, which he has difficulty holding onto. She holds the pad for him as he struggles and produces a scribble. He looks at it and seems to sigh, as much as one can with a tube snaked down their throat.

His weakness astounds her. She has known him as strong, and seeing him in this feeble state breaks off a small slice of her soul.

The pen slips out of his hand a few more times before he manages, with her help, to write a word. He is exhausted from the task. He drops his arm, as if he had been holding up the entire universe.

166

The pen falls from his hand and crashes to the floor, and she rushes to pick it up, absently pocketing the small pad as she chases the pen as it rolls away like a stubborn child who runs from a parent.

She almost runs into a team of caregivers as they enter the room. Quickly, she collects the pen and is annoyed that they have disturbed her in the paltry hour they have allowed her to see him.

"Visiting hours have been over for a while," one lab-coated asshole points out.

She explains that she has cleared it with the administrator, whose name inconveniently escapes her.

"Are you family?" they inquire further.

She explains herself to no avail. They tell her she can come back the next day, but they can't possibly let her stay. Her instinct is to put up a fight, and she doesn't want to leave, but this is his care team, so she capitulates.

She moves bedside and kisses him. "I will be back when they let me."

He opens his tired eyes and gives her a vague nod and gives a wisp of a squeeze with his weak hands. She feels as if he doesn't want her to go but can't be sure if it's her projecting the notion.

She kisses him again and thanks the team, asking when he may come off ventilator.

"We will know more after we examine him."

She nods and leaves, defeated. She negotiates the hallways of the hospital absently until she finds herself sitting in the parking lot in her idling car. She is crying.

That's when she feels something underneath her and she remembers the notepad that she had shoved in her back pocket. When she takes out the pad and reads the word, she cries even harder.

She looks at it and touches it as if trying to conjure him through the scribble on the page.

She looks at the paper adoringly, reading it in her mind repeatedly. It reads "Wife."

<h1 style="text-align:center">fifty eight</h1>

the next day, she is allowed in without having to create a scandal. He is still on the machine but seems more aware. She knows he is feeling better when they are alone and his hand magically finds its way to her right breast.

She looks at him surprised, and he manages a sly smile.

"So, you are better?"

He nods weakly, yet he seems stronger, not that that was too hard to achieve. Since he had debilitated so rapidly, she is happy to see some sign of increased strength.

Once again, her visit is interrupted by a cadre of caregivers. They ask her politely to move so they can hover over him. They move his legs and arms.

They tell him, and by default her, that he needs to sit up. They are concerned that his lungs will fill with fluid. They ask if it's okay to prop him up in addition to using the adjustable bed for the same purpose.

The sound that comes from him as they help him up is disturbing and compounded by the ventilator tube.

"It's the broken ribs," they explain to her as she rushes to him reactively.

If pain had a facial expression, he was wearing a triple portion.

"Why?" she asks with a hint of anger.

"He has been lying like this for almost two weeks with lung damage. We know there is fluid already, and we don't want it to build up, because then we will have to drain it."

She looks at him in clear discomfort, which causes her own pain. She is overwhelmed with all of it. He thankfully reaches out for her comfort. She takes his hand, and the angst on his face softens. She realizes that she is his ballast.

"When can he get off the ventilator?"

"Hopefully tomorrow, or in the next few days, but making him sit up as much as possible is key to expediting."

She nods, knowing she will likely have to shepherd him through this pain. She doesn't stop to wonder how much she can absorb. She squeezes his hand, causing his brow to partially relax.

"What about nutrition? He looks like he might break."

He looks at her, confused, and that turns to frustration. He makes a wave in front of his face.

"He's getting electrolytes and fluids through IV. Once we get him off the vent, we will work on getting his weight back."

He waves again more nervously.

"Mirror?" she asks.

He nods.

"I don't suppose you guys have a handheld mirror handy?" she asks sheepishly.

They look at her as if she's asked to shoot up right then and there. She sighs in frustration and takes a picture with her phone.

"Listen, you have been through a lot."

He motions her impatiently, and she reluctantly hands him the device. He looks at what must feel like a stranger. It is almost as if he deflates when he lays eyes on his own image. He has seen some poor facsimile of himself, broken, just as she has seen.

She does not envy him and wonders why she allowed him to look but can't think of a way she could have avoided it.

He turns away from her, which is the most he can do with limited movement. It as if he thinks he doesn't deserve her in the condition he is in.

"You are going to get better. You were in a bad accident, and between that and the trauma of the surgery, you have been hammered. You are strong, or you would not have survived."

He nods vaguely, and she sees a tear run down his cheek. She takes his hand, and more tears come. She squeezes his hand, and the eye flow slows.

When they tell her she must leave, she is almost grateful. When she gets to her car, she is able to let loose the waterfall she had been holding back.

fifty-nine

if one could see them, one would think they were a couple in an argument. But no one can see them, and besides that, they sit in the audience of the Moulin Rouge. Champagne sits in front of them yet remains untouched.

The audience is rapt with the delights of the famed show. Yet the ethereal beings seem perpetually bored.

"Why Paris? We are always in Paris," her voice asks in his head.

"Because you like romance. You always have."

"Is it me? Feels like the same sights over and over again."

"We can go anywhere, Italy? Greece? The Caribbean?"

In his head, he hears a sigh but her facade doesn't even move.

"You pick."

This is a losing battle for him, and he knows it. If he says they stayed in Paris because he thought that's what she wanted, she will be annoyed, and if he says he has no idea where she will be less bored, that will be an issue, too.

"Let's finish the show and then go," he suggests.

"This show, or ours?"

"Either. Both."

He has flipped the script on her indecisiveness, which shouldn't bother a being of his nature, but is perhaps another remnant of his former humanness. He knows she prefers him to make decisions for them, but also wonders if it is a trap to say he did something wrong. More wisps of humanity long since gone, yet clearly he, and possibly she, are still tethered to it to some degree.

The thought perplexes him. He wonders if their little game has caused this existential crisis of sorts. He looks at his counterpart, but she is better at hiding herself, she always had been. It was if she knew she would become ethereal, even when she was human.

He thinks to ask her if she is ready to change venues but decides against it. Rather, he simply transports them. It would seem as if they haven't moved. They could be easily still sitting in the theater, and they are now sitting at a candle-lit table, staring out at the waves of the Aegean Sea in an old village called Ano Mera.

"Mykonos! You always have known what I want, even before I do!"

And he is pleased that she is satisfied.

sixty

they finally have decided to pull the tube. She finds out as she is coming to visit. It is almost uncanny how they are always poking and prodding him when she is there.

She wonders if it is fate intervening on his behalf. He is a self-admitted baby when it comes to anything done to him, but it is draining for her to see him suffer. She knows she must be the strong one.

He looks at her nervously as they tell him to relax. He is anything but, and it is painfully obvious.

"It's going to be okay," she says soothingly.

"We need to get in there," the nurse says, asking her to move.

She moves aside, and the nurse tells him to take one big breath in and to exhale when she says. He does as instructed, and they pull out the tube.

He seems to feel a combination of stress and relief, but when he tries to talk, nothing comes out.

"Yeah, you won't have a voice for a while, and we have to be slow on water and food intake."

She has moved almost automatically to his side and is holding his hand. He looks at her gratefully, as he seems to have rebounded from the shock of the removal.

"That's progress," she says hopefully.

The nurses ask her to move again while they give him a Q-tip-sized stick with a small sponge attached with water in it.

"Go slow, okay?" the nurse instructs.

He rubs his throat and tries to speak again.

"Give it a few days, voice should come back."

He nods, and they tell him they will be back, and he will have to start physical therapy.

She sits on his bed and holds his hand. "I guess I should enjoy the silence while it lasts."

They share a laugh, and it's the first moment of much needed levity.

The surgeon comes in and seems to get the jovial vibe.

"Great to have you off ventilator. I'd like to get you moving as soon as possible. Don't want that lung to get the idea it can't heal. Plus, there is a bit of fluid, we need to keep an eye on that."

The surgeon tells him he would like to inspect the surgical wound and seems pleased.

"The staples need to come out in a week or so."

He nods. She is glad to see that his energy is improved. Having the tube out of his throat must be a massive relief.

He tries to speak, and then when he realizes he cannot, he asks for pen using his hands. She goes to her backpack and sees the last note he wrote. It makes her a little emotional, which she tries to hide from him.

She hands him the pen and paper. He is steadier than the last time, and he writes "Thank you."

She starts to cry, and he shakes his head. She can't help it. All the emotion she has held in comes pouring out her face all at one time.

Then, he falls asleep. She sits with him for as long as they will allow and hopes he wakes but doesn't. He has had little sustenance, and his body is recovering from serious trauma, so it's not surprising he is exhausted.

For some reason, it occurs to her as she leaves that it may be a year before they can have sex again. She shrugs it off and leaves, texting him to say what happened and that she will be back the next day.

sixty-one

when she arrives the next day, he is being told that once he is stable, they need to move him to a rehab to get him mobile. He doesn't seem happy. When they leave, she asks him about it. He tells her that given all that has gone wrong, he questions if a rehab will help. Plus, it is in an old-age home.

"You won't be able to visit," he breaks the news, in almost a whisper.

"What?" she asks, suddenly alarmed.

"Covid protocol," he says, his voice still weak.

"How long will you be there?"

"Not sure. I guess they have to okay me to be home first," he tells her.

She feels anxious. She also hates how the idea of not seeing him, being able to watch over him, feels very wrong to her. How can she do that from afar?

"When will they send you?"

"I'm not sure. Once they get the staples out. Make sure I am okay for the next step. But we can talk every day. FaceTime, too. It's just temporary."

She nods and tries not to show her disapproval. "FaceTime, it's not the same."

"I know, I don't like it either, but it's the circumstances of the time we are in. We are lucky you get to come here; other hospitals are closed to visitors. Imagine people who have relatives who are dying?"

"You almost died!"

"But I didn't."

"You sure seemed close; I thought I might lose you."

For some reason, he hadn't understood what he meant to her. Sure, they had been friends, and now obviously more. She had refused to leave his side, even when it didn't look like he would make it. She wouldn't leave, even when it was probably in her best interest to do so.

It was suddenly overwhelming for him. She had taken responsibility for him and his life when she didn't have an obligation to do so. She was ride or die, something we all want and need, but it scared him to death, and he felt ashamed of this feeling that was engrained.

He loved her. He somehow always had. The mutual caring was imbedded from their friendship, but showing up like this was unprecedented. He honestly didn't know how he would have reacted had their positions be reversed. Now, he was obligated to the commitment she deserved and had earned. The question was if he would be able to do it.

He didn't want to be pushed, but the pressure was coming from him, not her. She just showed up.

"I didn't think I was that bad off," he admits. "I didn't think I was at the risk I ended up being. I'm sorry you had to go through that."

"Don't do it again."

"Really? It's so much fun to get crushed by a truck. You have no sense of adventure."

"If this is the kind of adventure you are into, you are out a second wife."

He looks at her perplexed.

"Oh boy, you don't remember?"

She sees the blank look on his face and pulls out the notepad on which he wrote "wife" and shows it to him.

"Right! Yes, I am sorry. I was in and out then."

"I'm just confused," she says.

"About?"

"Where's my ring?"

He laughs. "Indeed, where is the fucker?"

The laugh is partly out of nervousness.

The mood changes as the surgeon comes in. He is a bookish-looking man, which one appreciates in a trauma surgeon.

"You look better," he says.

"I feel better off the ventilator."

"Most do. Has PT been to see you?"

"Not yet," he admits.

"It's important you sit up and get up. We don't want more complications."

"No, we do not," she chimes in.

The surgeon looks at her with certain empathy. Just then, the announcement comes in that visiting hours are over. She frowns in dismay. She collects her things and kisses him before telling him she will be back tomorrow. She thanks the surgeon, as well.

"I can't emphasize the importance of sitting up and moving as much as possible."

"I understand. I will try my best."

"You still have catheter in, but I am a bit concerned about everything being in working order."

"What?"

"We discussed this before surgery. There is a good chance you are not able to get an erection."

"I'm pretty sure I ignored you then, and I'm doing it now."

"We just may want to monitor it, and maybe discuss with your girlfriend. She won't leave your side."

"I'm aware."

"She calls around the clock to make sure you are okay. Were you aware of that?"

"No, I wasn't. I mean, I got crushed and had you rummaging around in me. When should I worry?"

"Not yet, but I thought we should address it."

"Always full of good vibes, doc!"

The surgeon laughs and says he will check in the next day.

sixty-two

she is moving, and she wished she wasn't. The timing was bad. He had told her it was okay to take a day off from running around like a crazy person for him. She deserved it. She argued that soon they wouldn't be able to see each other at all once he goes to rehab. She was being needy, and he wasn't. This annoyed her.

She was more vulnerable than a man who had been crushed by a truck, wasn't ambulatory, and was destined for a long road to recovery, if he were ever to recover fully.

Regardless, her plans to move had been set in motion well before this had happened to him. She shouldn't feel guilty, yet she did. He said as much for her not to, knowing her almost better than she knew herself.

He texted her during the day, saying that they were watching the fluid in his lungs, and they still were concerned of buildup. Sitting up was hard, but necessary. He had five broken ribs, so moving, coughing, sneezing, or laughing was almost unbearable.

The truth was she was worried. He wasn't moving so much, and the lung/fluid situation sounded dangerous. The lung had collapsed and apparently wasn't getting back to normal. They might have to do a procedure where they put a drain in his lung. The good news with that was he would have to stay in the hospital longer, meaning she could see him.

How can I root for that? He hates being poked and prodded.

More guilt, alongside a helping of utter helplessness, made her feel more pathetic.

She distracted herself with moving boxes around the new space, hoping to correspond each box to each room. Sadly, in her haste, and angst, she hadn't marked some as she had intended.

She sighed and plopped down on her couch in a small space that was available to sit in. She stayed there, mushed by a box containing lord knows what. She looks at a picture of them on her phone that they took on Christmas eve. She thinks they are a cute couple.

Needy.

She calls him and suggests she come down and visits. He says that he would like to see her, but it's a forty-five-minute drive for an hour visit and that she can come the next day, when she is working a few minutes away anyway.

She knows he is making sense and chooses to listen.

"I can unpack some, I guess."

"Okay, see you tomorrow?"

"Definitely."

sixty-three

they sit atop the Church of Panagia Paraportiani. Their all-white outfits would make them blend in with the exterior of the edifice if anyone could actually see them lounging there.

They watch the humans below them taking pictures of the church and each other. Strangers help couples and groups take memorable photos that they could never achieve alone.

"I like your idea of separating them. For sure they will crash," she says.

"I think the opposite. They are not crashing."

"She is too needy, and he is too aloof. They have attraction, yes, but those proclivities don't work together. Inevitably they will scare each other off," she announces.

He just returns a sly smile, as if he knows something she does not.

"What?" she asks.

"Nothing, no, nothing at all," he responds.

"When will you do it? I can hardly wait to prove you wrong!"

"Soon, it will happen soon."

"I like it here. How is it you always know what I will want?"

He chuckles. "It's *not* that I do. It is that you do not."

She frowns in disdain. It is a rare moment of visible expression. These creatures have evolved to full interactions with limited emotional expense, yet still have a scant whisper of having been born from humanity.

These two particular creatures are too far removed from their earthly beginnings and are unlikely to know how to speak with their mouths, yet some expressions sneak out in certain betrayal unbeknownst to them.

"Mykonos was the perfect choice," she says.

"I know how picky you can be. I am thrilled that you approve."

"You are making fun of me?"

"Never!"

She is vaguely satisfied with his answer. He hardly knows what to do. She usually sits in a deeply dissatisfied state. He wonders if they are evolving somehow again but thinks it more an aberration.

"I wish to put our respective theories to the test," she says.

"Understood. Perhaps a few more roadblocks and then we can separate them, but you are wrong."

She turns to him, her disdain returned. He pays no mind as he watches the silly humans trying to get the perfect picture of themselves using selfie sticks.

He sighs. She joins him in watching the ridiculousness.

sixty-four

when she comes to visit, he is sitting in a chair next to the bed. He looks very uncomfortable, and he shifts in his seat when she enters, grimacing as he moves.

"You look miserable," she says, matter of factly.

"I know they said I have a crumbled pelvis, but the ribs hurt way worse," he admits.

She looks at the external hardware jutting out of him and realizes that he must be terribly uncomfortable and only explaining part of the misery.

As if on cue, a medical team enters. It is as if they know she is there and need to disrupt her limited visiting hours.

After cursory questions as to how he feels, they tell him that the fluid in his lungs is not dissipating as they had hoped. They will likely have to drain it.

She watches his face as they tell him they need to perform more procedures on him. It is as if they'd extracted his face of all its blood. He is ashen, and she can see the stress slam him, like being crushed by a steamroller.

"Are you sure about this?" he asks.

"We will keep an eye on it. Sitting the way you are now should help."

"It's not exactly comfortable," he says, pointing to the external hardware jutting out from the hospital gown.

"I'm sure, but if you want a shot at not needing the lung to be drained, you will need to sit up as much as possible."

The surgeon comes in for his regular check, hearing the last of the assessment. He speaks with the pulmonary team briefly before turning to him.

"I'm glad to see you up. Were you able to stand?"

"Ten whole seconds, but they want to drain my lung. Can I be moved to rehab if they do that?"

"No, we have to see how that lung does, and if you need draining, the procedure is done here and until it stabilizes."

He sighs, and she touches his hand in support.

"I can only echo what they said. Keep up with the PT and sit up as much as possible. The body isn't used to the trauma, or not moving around, so it all will help move the process forward. I'd like to get those staples out in a day or so."

His pale face became whiter. She was surprised that was possible.

"Does it hurt?"

"You will be fine," the surgeon assures.

The surgeon pats him on the shoulder and reiterates that sitting and standing is his way to recovery. When he nods in acknowledgment, the surgeon says he will be back in a day and leaves.

He slumps further in his seat, adjusting as he can to avoid the massive screws that hold together a stabilizing bridge, causing even more discomfort than they already do.

"I don't know how many more procedures and poking around I can take," he says dejectedly.

"It will be okay," she assures him.

"You are better at this kind of thing than I am."

"Pretty much everyone is."

He cracks a smile.

"At least you can laugh a little," she says.

"I'm crying on the inside."

"Laughing is great medicine," the physical therapist chimes in, hustling into the room.

"I hope you have a long stand-up routine," he quips.

"Can you sit longer? Or are you ready to get back into bed?"

"Bed, definitely bed."

She watches empathetically as he gingerly uses his upper body strength with the help of the therapist. His face contorts in ways it wasn't made to, and he slides on the bed with a painful yelp that makes her hurt, too.

"Be back tomorrow," says the therapist.

"Great," he responds with a hint of sarcasm.

"It must get easier," she encourages.

"Let's hope."

sixty-five

he can't sleep. he watches some shit reality show about twenty-somethings stuck on some island and not allowed to fuck. They are penalized prize money for any physical interactions starting with a kiss. It is mindless bullshit, but it helps pass the time.

It is hard to sleep in the hospital, as they check him every few hours and ask to take vitals. It has annoyed him to the point where he has asked them to stop. On occasion he lets them, but mostly wants to unlock the cheat code to them deeming him well enough to be left alone.

Some idiots on the show end up hooking up even though they know it's against the rules and costs the winners cash from the pot.

He thinks about what the surgeon said, about not being able to achieve erection. He can't exactly test it given the public nature of his accommodations. He also can barely move below the waist, and to top it all off, he is sure that, despite the sponge baths, he must stink. His hair is reminiscent of an abandoned bird's nest.

He is afraid to touch it, knowing it may be nothing but limp and useless. It isn't as if he could have sex now anyway, so why bother? But it did bother him. Why wouldn't it?

It's not as though watching these oversexed twenty-somethings is doing much for him anyway.

He thinks about texting her. Now he feels guilty over not mentioning the risk of never being able to achieve erection. It's not as

187

if it would have stopped him from heeding the recommendation of the surgeon. He had been in so much pain, he knew he had no choice. Instant gratification was born out of desperation, and he promptly told himself that wouldn't happen to him.

Let's hope.

He does text her. He tells her he appreciates everything she has done. To his surprise, she texts back.

You would do the same for me.

He wonders if he would. Sure, he would do something, but would he be as relentless about making sure she was okay?

I'm pretty sure you are a better person than I am.

Miss you.

Just then, some people come in and just flip on the light.

"Seriously? Turn that off!" he barks.

"Sorry, sorry," an outline of one of two people says.

"It's five in the morning," he points out.

"We have been sent to get an X-ray," the outline says.

"Lung?"

"Yes, can you sit up?"

"I have five broken ribs. I can't do much of anything," he responds.

"We will have to get this under you," outline tells him, holding up a square piece of metal.

"Great."

"May we help you up to do this?"

He isn't happy about it but agrees. They lift him up, and he yelps in pain as they do. It feels better when they lower him, but the metal is also uncomfortable.

"Can you hurry? This is very uncomfortable."

"We just have to get the right angle."

They finally finish then help him up again. It is somehow more painful than the first time.

"Can you tell me what you see?" he asks.

"Really a radiologist needs to confirm, but I can see some fluid."

"Enough to have to drain?"

"Not my lane, man," the outline says.

"Thanks."

The two leave, and he sees that she has texted some more, asking if he is okay.

He explains what has just happened, and she asks a litany of questions he can't answer.

I will see you during visiting hours. Any food I can bring?

Thanks, I haven't much appetite.

LMK if you change your mind.

sixty-six

"i'm bored," she says.

They stare at the Kato Mili Windmills and the blue sea beyond them. Tourists move in and out of their sightline. He realizes that his eternal partner seems to come with little to no attention span or patience.

"Did you find Paris more exciting?"

"It's our project. It's lagging."

"We must let it take its course. If we interfere too much, we are merely playing chess with human pieces."

"I thought that was the point!" she exclaims.

"Perhaps we should go back to Paris? Rome? New York? LA? London?"

"London? You know I find the food bland!"

He chuckles at the notion.

"You always choose best," she encourages.

"You liked it here initially!"

She looks at him for a few moments and then returns her attention to the windmills. He hears a muffled sigh from her in his head.

"Maybe just a few more obstacles? Make it harder for them?"

"What would you have me do? This is a serious test for both."

"Maybe a side project?"

It is his turn to sigh.

"We all have our limitations, even we do. For all we know, we are marionettes made to dance on strings," he says.

"How can that be?"

"I just think it possible. Perhaps there are beings that are playing us, just as we are with them."

"You are annoyingly smarter than I," she admits.

"No, we just think differently. But I do think a change of venue is in order."

sixty-seven

he orders a milk shake. He feels he deserves it. The pain in his side where they have inserted a drainage tube is starting to kick in, as whatever anesthetic they gave him wears off.

She texts him, upset. The procedure has once again cut into her limited visiting hours, and she knows he didn't want the procedure.

The nurse brings the milkshake, and in the first moment of chocolatey delights, he forgets where he is. In fact, he forgets everything.

Chocolate solves real problems.

She texts him again and says she will be there the next day and asks if they said they will move him to the rehab. He tells her that they must get the lung stabilized and the surgical staples out first. It will be a few days.

He is glad that part is over, but for some reason, he knows he isn't out of the woods yet. He can't walk, and there is now a tube in his lung. He looks at the companion collection box that has some blood-colored fluid in it.

That's it? This is why you did this to me?

The pain at the point of procedure, for some reason, hurts more. The surgeon comes in and, per usual, asks how he is doing and then tells him the staples will come out in a day or so.

"Can't wait!"

"You'll be fine."

"That's what I was told about the drain."

"See you tomorrow."

The surgeon leaves, and he finishes his milkshake, wondering if the poking and prodding will ever end. The pain is amplified, despite being on pain medication.

He is full from the milkshake, as they never let him eat or drink before any procedure. His appetite hasn't been much through this anyway, and he doesn't move, which makes him insane. He is too much in his own head and he knows it.

She texts him and asks what food she can bring him. When he does eat, he has found the hospital offerings only worsen his appetite.

I don't know, he texts back.

Thai?

Can I let you know tomorrow?

Sure.

She is always engaging him, even though he is laid up with time on his hands and she hasn't much to spare. Yet she makes time for him. She is showing who she is, without ever being asked.

Ride or die.

When he thinks on it, he realizes that this is who anyone would want to be with. When the shit hits the fan, a person who is unwavering, who does not hesitate, is who we all need in our respective corners.

A cadre of medical staff comes in and they move to the drain and look at the collection box. They pick it up so he can see. There isn't so much fluid, but it is a disturbing blood-brown color.

"I thought there would be more considering the urgency."

"It drips slowly, but rest assured, it needed to be done."

Of course.

"We will be back tomorrow. Hopefully it will be all set in a few days, and we can get you to the rehab. In the meantime, same recommendation: PT, sit up as long as possible."

He nods and is grateful when they don't linger.

sixty-eight

"ow!"

"That bad?" the person removing the surgical staples asks.

"Not good," he retorts.

"You want me to stop?" she asks.

"How many more?"

"About ten."

"Fuck's sake," he says. "Just be gentle."

She gives him a break before painfully plucking the remainder of the staples out. The surgeon materializes mid-pluck.

"I see you are enjoying yourself," the surgeon quips upon entering.

"Yes, you know how to show a guy a good time."

He yelps as the last staple comes out and wonders if these people were all medieval torturers in past lives.

"All done," she says, making room for the surgeon.

"How am I looking?"

"I'm pleased with the healing," he says, noticing the collection box.

"Not much output for having to stab in the lung. Makes me wonder if it was necessary."

"It was," the surgeon reassures him.

"Can we be done with all the poking around in me please?"

"That's the plan."

"Try and stick to it. I'm not sure how much more I can take."

The surgeon nods empathetically. As he leaves, the physical therapist comes in.

"Ready to get up?"

"I have this attachment," he says, pointing to the collection box.

"Don't worry, it's portable."

He struggles to get to the edge of the bed, eschewing help offered, insisting he must do it on his own. It takes forever and the external hardware jabs him as he sits as upright as someone in his condition can. The therapist gives him the walker, and he does three sets of assisted standing for roughly ten seconds each. Then they use a board to slide him into the chair. It's brutal—sitting, an otherwise remedial task, is ridiculously painful.

She comes in with food in hand. The therapist says he will be back in forty-five minutes or so to get him back into bed.

She kisses him, and he worries that days of sponge bath only has left him with that not-so-fresh smell. She says nothing about it, even when he brings it up.

"Did they say when they will send you to the rehab?"

"I have to get this out first," he says, pointing to the collection box. "A few days is my guess."

"Are you sure they don't allow visitors?"

"Yes, but I have little choice, I need to at least be able to use a walker to get around."

"I don't like it."

"I can't go home like this, and the hospital can only keep me for so long."

She nods. "They say when you can go home?"

"When I have enough strength to get upstairs safely. Apparently, they have a practice flight."

She wonders whether her discomfort is obvious to him.

"Are you hungry?" she asks, holding the bag of food.

"Will you eat with me?"

She nods and procures a pasta Bolognese. He eats a small portion and then stops.

"That's it?" she asks between mouthfuls.

"Yes, babe, I get full quickly. I guess not moving so much, I don't need the energy I usually do."

"I don't know how much more I can take," she admits.

"No one could blame you."

"Maybe they will change the rules at the rehab and I can visit?"

"Let me get there first. I'm here for a few more days."

He watches as she picks at the food, mind obviously in hurricane speed thoughts. He wonders if it will bring her some relief not to feel mandated to show up every day, having to check on him, watch over him. He wonders if he will be relieved she doesn't have the burden.

sixty-nine

they sit atop the Statue of Liberty. He is enamored by the stunning skyline, while she is unable to sit still.

"There is no one to judge from here," she says.

"True, but the view is unreal."

She sighs. "So, our experiment is unwatchable, and now this."

"Our experiment is still operating. I'm sure it will kick into another gear shortly. You don't enjoy the suffering? I thought you might."

"There is too much suffering, not enough death."

"If there were death, the experiment would be over."

She shrugs nonchalantly.

"Soon they will be separated, and we can throw in some new obstacles for them to negotiate."

"Except death."

"Right, there will be no death."

She edges off the iconic statue and falls into the night sky. He watches, unimpressed, knowing that she cannot die, and that she means only to prove a point. He decides to go after her. It is of little consequence to him, either, other than she can't accuse him of leaving her alone.

<h1 style="text-align:center">seventy</h1>

four hospital administrators surround his bed with their arms crossed.

"Unfortunately, we can't keep you much longer," one says.

"Yes, you mentioned that before they needed to drain the lung."

"That has been done. We have to get you to the rehab."

"What about the pus coming out of the surgical wound?"

"It's normal."

"Then send me off, if that's what you need to do."

"Unless home is an option, but we don't recommend it."

"You guys are the experts. When will this happen?"

"Soon."

"It's just that my girlfriend won't be able to visit, and I'd like to let her know."

"Understood," one says before they all parade out of the room.

He texts her to let her know, and naturally, she asks when it will happen. All he can say is what they told him.

She isn't happy but says she will be in to see him during the limited visiting window. A new face enters. He says he will see her later, that someone has come to poke him undoubtedly.

The medic does ask to see his surgical wound, and when he does, he echoes what the administrators told him.

Normal.

The medic cleans and dresses the wound. He thanks him and the man leaves.

Doesn't seem normal. None of this does.

The next day, they move him to the rehab. It is essentially an old-age home. He has been reduced to similar circumstances. He can't get out of bed to use the bathroom. He struggles to get the bedpan under him between his injuries and the hardware, not to mention the loss of strength. It is a messy endeavor, and debilitating.

The new place, although called a rehab, does less PT than the hospital. He wants to push and get up. In a week, he is supposed to be transported to the surgeon's office to hopefully get external hardware removed.

She texts and calls, calls, and texts, voicing her frustration and concern. He does his best to keep her sane.

He lucks into getting a Covid shot by virtue of being a resident at an old-age home. One benefit of the accident is an early vaccination, where otherwise he would have been ineligible.

The pus keeps coming, and he takes a picture and texts the surgeon.

Normal, he texts back.

He wonders if that's all anyone ever says. Seems clear it is not normal at all.

He is getting stronger. He is determined despite the discomfort of the outer hardware.

The food is horrible, so he leans on Grub Hub for sustenance. He gets his vaccination and spends time reading when he is not getting physical therapy. For a supposed rehab, he gets very little. They provide an hour per day. But in reality, it is less. They get him in and out of the chair, so he takes it upon himself to request assistance standing with walker, or getting back into the chair a few more times. This seems to annoy the staff, but he can't do it without them, and his desire to get back moving trumps that.

They inform him that he can't go to the surgeon, because of Covid concerns, but when he texts the surgeon with that news, he says he will handle it.

The wound keeps draining, and it begins to have an odor. They clean it and dress it, but the wound doesn't seem to care.

He texts the surgeon again, showing him pictures of the pus oozing out of the wound.

He texts back that he will look at the appointment.

When he mentions it to some staff at the rehab, they tell him he can't go. Again, the universal excuse: Covid.

He passes this on to the surgeon, who seems annoyed and tells him not to worry and that he will make it happen.

He texts her and tells her he is frustrated. He can't take care of himself, and the old-age home doesn't help much. It's a shithole. *Rehab* is a loosely based term, given that it's less time rehabbing, and he must push them to get him moving.

The day comes when he is scheduled to be transported to surgeon's office. He is taken by gurney in and out of the ambulance and laid in a waiting room before being painful being moved to a hard X-ray table. Thankfully, the external hardware can come out.

No more twelve-inch screws coming out of my body.

He asks the surgeon to look at wound, and when he does, his face contorts in a disturbing fashion.

"What is it?" he asks.

"Hush!" the surgeon reacts, annoyed.

He sighs.

"This is infected. We need to operate."

For fuck's sake.

"What? No, I can't take anymore."

"It has to be done."

"When?"

"I will admit you to hospital today, and as soon as it can be scheduled, we will go in."

He has a bad feeling about it. Perhaps he has just had too much. He had time to mentally prepare for the first surgery. Now he has none and he is scared.

"I have no fever. Are you sure?"

"Yes."

seventy-one

he orders another milkshake. This is now the post-procedure ritual. He is hooked up to what seems like a thousand tubes, a drain, and an IV comes out on both sides of him.

The surgeon visits him and says that they had to send samples to an infectious disease specialist, and that they will need to keep him on IV antibiotics for a while. The tubes are there to stay for at least six weeks. The good news is that he doesn't have to go back to rehab, and therefore she can see him again.

She has had to look at this semblance of a person for weeks now and still stays.

He nods dejectedly.

The days pass, all the same. He manages the physical therapy with the IV, which is staying with him until he can safely take oral antibiotics. Then eventually, more surgery to get hardware out.

Weeks later, he can get home. The recovery is slow and painful, but she is there as much as she can be.

Ride or die.

He hates himself for not being self-sufficient. He can provide nothing; he does nothing except try to regain some semblance of what he was.

He wonders how close to death he was, or if it would have been better off if he didn't make it. So much suffering for him, and for her, and for what? The depression weighs on him, as nurses and therapists come and go to change his IV and try and get him moving.

He makes his way with a walker. The threat of a fall scares her to death. He is feeble, so it is understandable.

He misses Saigon. He is with friends until he is in condition to care for him. It is a month away, which is two months too long.

The days pass, and he gets better. IV out, stitches out, he makes his way without the walker and even gets to the gym to get some strength back.

He heals but not completely. There is no retuning to pre-accident condition. But what was gained easily outdoes what was lost.

Ride or die.

She heals, too, but the ghost of what she went through does still haunt her. Regardless, it has brought them closer, and she is grateful. He knows that she is an immoveable force that will back him up in the worst of conditions.

In the end, you can't ask for more than the dependability of those who go through the worst of the worst with you. That may be the most valuable of all human commodities—not gold, or mansions, or fancy clothes. It is dependability.

seventy-two

they sit atop the Freedom Tower. The cityscape is different from the last but just as impressive. She stares out at the urban beauty, and oddly for her, says nothing. He looks at her, as the silence is off-putting.

Their comfortable white clothes seem almost painted on even as the wind blows. They do not move at the frenetic pace of the city below them. They are the eye of the storm.

"They both live?" she asks finally.

"They do."

"They experience no conflict?"

"Of course they do."

"What did we find out?"

"You tell me," he suggests.

"I don't know. They didn't seem like run-of-the-mill humans."

"True, they don't. What else?"

"There is something, but I can't quite put my finger on it."

He turns to her and smiles wickedly.

"What have you done?"

"Nothing," he responds.

She is flummoxed. She knows there is something afoot.

There is something.

Of course, he can hear her thoughts.

"Shit," she says.

Shit, indeed.

They watch their experiment as if they are fast-forwarding. They see him moving with a walker or crutches. She dotes on him. He wants to do everything. She doesn't let him. He tells her he needs to work harder to get back together. She still won't let him, but when she is not looking, he does what he wants regardless.

They get along well. On occasion, they butt heads, as both are stubborn, but the accident and subsequent repercussions have brought them closer. They resolve quickly, and he credits their friendship, which made the relationship bond stronger. She hates that he thinks of them as still friends, but he quells that notion by telling her the friendship makes the romance better.

They witness a full recovery, they move in together, and he proposes. Not surprisingly, she says yes. They have weathered a lot, and there are more life obstacles to negotiate, but they are battle tested. They get beaten down, but they lift each other up. They survive to fight another day, but Father Time remains undefeated.

They stare out at the city as if they are watching the tail credits to a movie that affected their core.

"It all seems familiar," she says, breaking their silence.

"It should."

"Wait, can it be?"

"Yes."

"This is why you couldn't change anything?"

"Yes."

"Those humans were us?"

"Yes."

"Why did you show it to me?"

He looks at her. This is the question he has been wanting to answer. The wind blows gently, the day is as perfect as can be, and he tells her.

9 798218 139490